AQUA E ROTICA 2

12 Stories / No Boundaries

AQUA EROTICA 2

12 Stories / No Boundaries

A MELCHER MEDIA DURABOOK

MELCHER
MEDIA

Published in the UK by Dorling Kindersley Limited
80 Strand, London WC2R 0RL
www.dk.com
in association with

 MELCHER MEDIA

124 West 13th Street
New York, NY 10011
www.melcher.com

Publisher: Charles Melcher
Associate Publisher: Bonnie Eldon
Editor in Chief: Duncan Bock
Project Editor: Megan Worman
Production Director: Andrea Hirsh

Designed by Elizabeth Van Itallie
Cover photograph by Patrik Rytikangas
Cover model: Sabrina Sikora

Copyright © 2005 Melcher Media, Inc.

All rights reserved. No part of this publication may be reproduced, stored in a
retrieval system, or transmitted in any form or by any means, electronic, mechanical,
photocopying, recording, or otherwise, without prior consent of the publishers.

DuraBook™, patent no. 6,773,034, is a trademark of Melcher Media, Inc. The
DuraBook™ format utilizes revolutionary technology and is completely waterproof
and highly durable.

09 08 07 06   10 9 8 7 6 5 4 3

Printed in China

A CIP catalogue record for this book is available from the British Library.

ISBN-13: 978-1-59591-008-0
ISBN-10: 1-59591-008-5

First Edition

TABLE OF CONTENTS

TOO NICE A PERSON

Thomas S. Roche

ere's the place: a Victorian flat, second floor, third if you count the garage, on a steep hill overlooking a fog bank. Outside, there's a funky façade, windows double-paned beneath carved wooden gargoyles. Inside, behind those double-paned windows, ornate window trim peeks around black fabric from Wal-Mart, 99 cents per yard, pinned in the corners to protect the neighbors (who, on this street just west of Castro, could probably handle anything). The hardwood floors were recently refinished. Cheap rugs cover them in $29.99 luxury. The room where it happens used to be a formal dining room. French doors open onto the living room, until the sobbing begins, when she's going to close them to keep the cats out.

She stands, shadow-cut against standing IKEA halogens, brushed aluminum snaking in obscene curves and pouring white-yellow onto her back, illuminating her from behind. The rubber skirt shimmers in that yellowish glare. If you were standing between her and those halogens, you'd see the high slit in the back of the skirt, her legs spread slightly to open it and show off her inner thighs almost to the point of indecency. If you got closer—that is, if she *let* you—you would see the sheen of moisture trickling down those thighs, soaking the lace tops of her stockings. You'd see the same moisture running down the small of her back underneath the hem of the tight rubber halter—for this is sweat, the sweat of excitement, not the moisture of her cunt, which doesn't run down her thighs, only because she's wearing a cotton thong underneath the tight rubber skirt.

"Hurt him," she says, her voice steeped in evil, the kind of gleeful desire for mayhem that populates the minds of fantasists in lonely beds everywhere.

The girl's hands shake as she looks at the Dominant.

She's a boyish plain Jane with horn-rimmed glasses—not really a girl, but younger than the Dominant, and feeling younger every second.

In fact, Holly is twenty-nine, her hair short and bottle-blonde but with little electric-blue frosting on the tiny set of bangs. She looks boyish except for the ample hips and breasts, shrouded by a PVC thong and halter. She is short but totters on the three-inch heels of her knee-high patent-leather boots—$139.95 somewhere on Haight. Or was it mail order from Hot Topic? She never can remember where she gets stuff.

The cane that quivers in her hand is also PVC, of a sort, a slim and heavy synthetic implement far from the Victorian birch-rods of Holly's favorite porn novels. She knows it hurts on her ass; she's hit herself with it a hundred times, sprawled naked on her lonely bed, legs spread, back and arm twisted at improbable angles to give her some decent swing space, face buried in the pillow to hide her screams from the neighbors.

Holly's eyes flicker from the Dominant to the submissive, who is bent over a spanking bench, his ankles cuffed to one set of sturdy wooden legs, his wrists to the other. His genitals have been wrapped in white rope and forced back between his legs, attached to the strut of the spanking bench. The alabaster nylon is pulled so tight that his balls swell, distended, and his hard cock pulses with fullness. His face is twisted in an expression of fear, his small goatee and mustache flecked with spittle as he breathes very, very hard, moaning between great gulping breaths.

"Please," he whimpers. "Please, Holly, don't."

It brings her back from her fear, stays the quivers in her hands, to hear her name said like that.

It brings the Dominant back, too, and she is across the room in an instant, grabbing Caleb's face, squeezing it in her hand as he whimpers.

"You don't call her that!" growls the Dominant. "You call her Mistress."

"Sorry, sorry," he grunts.

The Dominant's hand comes back, swings forward in a motion so fluid it's clear she's done it a million times. This time, though, it's Caleb on the receiving end, and Holly utters a little whimper of sympathy as she sees his body jerking with the slap.

Her hand tangled in his longish hair, the Dominant just looks at him with her eyes wide, her lips tight.

"Sorry, Mistress," he gasps as she draws back her hand. "I'm sorry, Mistress," he blurts.

She gives him another slap, just for good measure, then releases his hair, turns on her four-inch heel and stalks back across the room.

"Hurt him," says the Dominant. "He needs it."

Holly can feel her heart pounding, her head spinning. She hesitates, looks at the Dominant, and feels the surge of fear that comes from the possibility of displeasing the older woman. She creeps toward the boy.

Caleb is not a boy; in fact, he is far from it. Still, Holly has always referred to him, around her friends, as "the boy." In the beginning, it allowed her to talk about him without using one of the emotionally charged terms she might have used—"boyfriend," "lover," "guy I'm seeing," "guy I'm sleeping with," "guy who says maybe he'll let me tie him up and slap the shit out of him." Since she thinks of herself as a girl, it always just seemed right.

In fact, a nervous gent like Caleb, pretty to a fault, successful in early life—he was freakin' captain of the football team, for God's sake, passed the Bar on the first damn try, became a junior partner at twenty-eight—is probably old enough to be ripe for his first mid-life crisis, and who knows? He's the type who might have shown up in this very dungeon with a wad of Franklins and a guilty look on his face. The Dominant has seen it a million times. Lawyers always have guilty looks on their faces.

Except that if Caleb hadn't met Holly, he would never, ever be here. Not out of guilt, or fear of being discovered, but because he just . . . wouldn't.

But he did meet Holly, who is less of an alpha-whatever, less successful in early life despite a bachelor's from Brown. She's not a junior partner in anything, has no law degree, and is not in possession of stacks of hundreds to carry around with a guilty look. She's spent most of her adult life working in a library and wishing they carried more Victorian porn. She keeps meaning to get back to school so she can apply for a senior librarian position and make another $3.65 an hour, but in the meantime, she likes that at the Castro branch things go slow enough that she always has time to sneak a little de Sade between patrons. "She's a little underemployed," her mom is fond of saying, "and that's fine." Caleb's always had such a thing for librarians, though, bookish little closet sluts who rub themselves to books called *Incest* and *Rape* in between shifts, that he doesn't seem to think she's under-anything— and while we're at it, the hundreds may be his but they're in Holly's purse.

And here they both are, and Caleb is simpering.

"Please, Mistress," squeaks Caleb as Holly nears him. "Please, baby—please, darling, please don't!"

Holly glances at the Dominant again; the look on the woman's face makes Holly take a deep breath and round Caleb's body, seizing his hair.

She gets a good grip on his hair—she's done *that* before, after all—but her first slap is tentative, weak. Caleb responds as if she's punched him full in the face; he wails softly and then whimpers, "I mean Mistress. I'm sorry, Mistress, please don't hurt me!"

Holly slaps him harder, surprised at herself. She stares into his eyes and sees them moist with swiftly forming tears.

So enraptured by those tears is Holly that she doesn't notice the Dominant's footsteps as she approaches Holly's left elbow.

"I think he's begged enough," says the Dominant, holding up a complicated array of straps and buckles that culminates in a three-inch, flesh-colored dildo. "Gag him."

Holly takes the gag from the Dominant. The Dominant holds Caleb's hair as Holly arranges the buckles, and when Caleb won't open his mouth the Dominant goads Holly into slapping him again. Still, Caleb won't open his mouth, so the Dominant grabs his cheeks and squeezes.

Finally Caleb's mouth pops open, a plaintive wail escaping, and Holly gingerly puts the dildo in. His tongue tries to force it out; after a moment, she gets frustrated and shoves.

Holly hears Caleb gagging on the dildo as the Dominant helps her get the straps around his head. The two of them pull the buckles tight, and Caleb's pleas are now nothing more than gurgling, grunting moans of dismay.

The Dominant leans over Caleb, takes Holly's hair in her hands, and gently kisses her on the lips, her tongue trailing against Holly's ever so slightly. Holly feels a faint tingle go through her body.

"Now hurt him," says the Dominant.

Caleb's face is turned to the side so he can look at Holly. His eyes are locked on hers; they say everything his mouth cannot. *Please don't hurt me, Holly. I love you. Don't you love me? If you hurt me I'll leave you. If you hurt me I'll hate you. If you hurt me I'll hurt, and you don't want that, do you?*

Holly breaks eye contact with what feels like a yank. She comes around behind, looking at his ass and his tormented cock between his spread legs. She breathes hard as she raises the cane.

Caleb tenses against the strike. She expects the cane to make a whizzing sound as it comes down; it always does when she hits herself with it. But in the air it makes no sound at all; Holly is swinging it too slowly. There is only the faint, dull thump of it striking Caleb's ass. Caleb, however, makes a sound, a soft, muffled wail from behind the cock-shaped gag.

"Harder," says the Dominant, her hand tweaking Caleb's nipple clamps. "Much, much harder."

Holly draws back and strikes again. This time she gets a satisfying whizzing sound, but the thump against his thighs is not as loud as Holly expects. Hitting Caleb is very different than hitting herself. Caleb's body, nonetheless, jerks and twists in his bonds. He whimpers behind the gag.

Seated in front of the spanking bench with Caleb's face cradled in her lap, the Dominant draws her long nails down his back, leaving vicious red streaks. She sneers. "I said harder!" she shouts angrily.

Driven on by the rising fury of the Dominant, Holly draws back and brings the cane down swiftly, not even thinking this time. Caleb screams—the sound becoming nothing but a muffled groan as it shudders through the gag. Holly strikes his ass again, and Caleb writhes.

"Harder," says the Dominant, and bends her face down close to Caleb's.

Holly wonders if Caleb can smell her. Holly smelled her earlier, during the kiss, the scent of female sweat and Dr. Bronner's lavender. But Caleb's face is in her lap—can he smell her cunt? Is the Dominant turned on? As turned on as Holly is?

Holly strikes him harder.

"Faster," says the Dominant. "Keep hitting his ass until I tell you to stop. Then you're going to work on his balls."

Holly's heart pounds in her chest, her breath coming short as she lays a swift series of blows up Caleb's thighs, struggling to maintain her balance as Caleb swirls and thrashes on the bench. She's striking him harder now, and the stripes begin to appear. Angry red crisscrosses lead from the fleshy part of his upper thigh up over his ass, then down again, very close to the swollen, bound balls in their white nylon prison.

Holly can feel her nipples getting hard.

Caleb is sobbing now, his cheeks moist with tears as he struggles against his bonds, trying to escape the quickening blows of the cane. Holly moves faster, hits harder, listens to him choke back sobs behind the gag. Her eyes widen. She can feel beads of sweat popping out all over her back. She grits her teeth and moves forward, striking him more fully with the cane. She hits him faster and listens to him sob. She knows her pussy is wet.

"Harder," coos the Dominant, clearly pleased for the first time tonight. Holly draws back the cane and obeys.

Caleb wraps his fingers around the chains that suspend

the sling. He grips them hard as Holly lays into his thighs, her clit swelling and throbbing against the tight PVC thong as she watches the angry red stripes appear. A bead of moisture escapes the synthetic material and creeps down her thigh, making her shiver.

She lunges forward and grabs his cock and balls with her free hand, yanking. Caleb groans.

"Not until I tell you, dear," says the Dominant, her voice rich with pleasure as she caresses Caleb's face. "Not until I tell you."

Holly steps back and lifts the cane again. Caleb's ass and upper thighs are a crisscross of magenta streaks, and when she starts again Holly does everything but play tic-tac-toe on them. She hits him so hard she can feel the impact going up her arm and into her body. It feels like it's rumbling right to her clit, and she tenses her thighs hungrily, which only makes her totter more precariously on the high heels.

She hears herself growling. Her hand becomes a blur as she strikes Caleb faster and faster. Caleb has long since stopped writhing; he has become a mass of shuddering flesh, bound to the sling, twitching with each blow. Holly winds up and brings her arm down with the hardest blow yet.

That gets him writhing again.

"Very good," sighs the Dominant as she caresses Caleb's chest. "Now grab his balls and pull."

Holly pounces, dropping the cane, crouching down with her high heels planted between Caleb's knees. She grabs Caleb's bound genitals and slowly pulls them, listening to the bound boy moan, then groan, then shriek as she twists and tugs at them. The Dominant caresses his harnessed face, smiling at Holly.

"Slap them," she says. "And slap his cock, too."

Holly slaps Caleb's balls with her hand, harder than she means to. Caleb jerks and trembles all over. She wraps one hand around his cock and slaps it with the other. He trembles some more, muffled sobs coming once again.

Holly slaps his hard cock some more, spanking it back and forth as Caleb pulls against his bonds. Another bead of moisture escapes her thong and runs all the way down to her thighs. She grips Caleb's prick firmly and slaps harder, her face reddening with the effort and her cleavage growing pink with arousal.

Holly is so used to giving hand jobs, and so turned on, that she doesn't even realize she's stroking his cock as she slaps it. Her hand moves up and down rhythmically, and after the first thirty blows, she can feel the first pulse of hot fluid on her hand. She's so turned on she doesn't care, or maybe she does. She grips him harder and starts slapping his cock at the head—the most sensitive part.

Caleb groans and arches his back. A hot stream erupts from his cock and covers Holly's shoes. He thrashes back and forth as he comes. Holly keeps spanking his cock with one hand, her other hand jerking him off. The combined sensation makes him come hard, and jets of cum cover Holly's shoes and hands.

The Dominant does not pull away but continues stroking Caleb's face. She smiles.

Holly stops slapping Caleb's cock. She is breathing very

hard. The feel of his cum on her hands is exciting to her. More beads of moisture escape her thong.

"Do you know what happens to submissives who come before their mistresses do?"

Caleb's eyes go wide and frightened as the Dominant unbuckles his head harness and pulls the cock out of his mouth. A long string of drool glistens in the IKEA halogens.

She beckons to Holly. Holly comes around to Caleb's head and the Dominant tips his head back with her hand twisted in his hair. With her other hand, the Dominant grabs Holly's wrist and shoves her fingers into his mouth. He accepts them obediently, licking his own cum from her fingers. When Caleb has cleaned Holly's hands, Holly shoves her fingers roughly in to his mouth and feels a surge of excitement as she feels him gagging.

The Dominant cocks her head at Holly and then glances at Holly's shoes. Holly feels a wave of excitement. The Dominant eases Caleb's head out of her lap and leaves it lolling there at the edge of the spanking bench. She shoves the chair back, and Holly takes her place standing at Caleb's head.

She lifts one foot, plants it on the edge of the spanking bench.

"Clean them," she growls, feeling heat rise in her cunt as she says it.

Caleb begins licking his cum from his mistress's boots. Holly watches him as best she can, but his rumpled hair hides much of what he's doing. Through the leather, she can feel the warm stroke of his tongue against her toes. The feeling excites her. Every time she catches a glimpse of his red tongue slipping out to caress the patent leather, lapping his own cum off her boots, Holly feels a pulse go through her clit.

She switches shoes, letting the now-obedient Caleb clean more of his cum. He does so without resistance. Holly admires the glistening sheen of her boots in the halogen light. The Dominant has vanished into the other room, and when she returns, Holly's eyes go a bit wide and her boyish face gains a quizzical expression.

The Dominant smiles.

"I figured you'd want to get off now," she said, glancing down at the enormous strap-on jutting from her naked body. "While I rape the little fucker's ass."

Holly's thighs turn into jelly at the sound of that word: *rape*. That's what this is, rape. Force. Nonconsensuality. They're forcing him. Caleb's head tips back, and Holly sees his frightened eyes, terror flickering in them as he tries to assess whether the Dominant is being serious, whether Holly, his mistress, will really let this happen, let his asshole be desecrated by this cruel, vicious stranger, a woman who plainly does not care whether he wants it or doesn't want it.

But then, regardless, there is no question about whether Holly wants to get off.

"Yes," says Holly to the Dominant. "Rape the little bitch."

Caleb only squirms a little; it hurts for him to move, Holly did such a good job on his ass. For the most part, he merely whimpers pathetically as the Dominant stalks across the room to take her place at his unplumbed entrance.

Holly strips off her PVC thong over her boots. The synthetic fabric glistens with moisture. A little surprised at herself, she rubs it all over Caleb's face, and he obediently laps at the juice-slick fabric.

"See what you did to me, you little bitch?" she sighs. "You got me all wet."

Holly has surprised herself by saying that, but the sound of it feels good in her mouth. She tosses the thong onto the small of Caleb's back and pulls over the low chair. She plants herself in front of Caleb's face, her naked ass shoved far forward on the edge of the chair. She spreads her legs very wide, so they're bent over the arms of the chair.

She hasn't shaved; she hasn't even trimmed. Normally she can't get head without at least running a trimmer through her hair; something about having an unshaved cunt makes her feel too demanding. She had a friend who once told her that pubic hair traps tastes and smells, so it's more pleasant to give head when the woman's trimmed or shaved. That thought has always nagged at her, making her spend a little extra time in the bathroom when she thought such a thing might be a possibility.

But this time, there was too much to do—and to be honest, she didn't even think about it. Her hair now is full, shrouding her sex in a wiry bush she couldn't even wear to the beach.

But there's no time to worry about that, because if Holly doesn't come soon she is going to fucking scream. Caleb looks up at her with frightened and excited eyes, and she grabs his hair and roughly shoves his face into her crotch.

Caleb descends on Holly's cunt with a ferocity that frightens her a little—at first. His tongue swirls around her clit and hungrily delves down into her cunt. Her eyes go wide as she feels his nimble member teasing her sensitive flesh. She's close to coming already.

But when she feels Caleb's body tense against the entrance of the Dominant's cock, that's when she can't hold it back anymore.

She tries to stifle her cries of orgasm, because she doesn't want to be the one who ends the scene, and she doesn't want it to be over yet. But she can't stop the moans, her mouth popping open wide as she cries out in a climax that leaves her shuddering and dizzy.

"That's one," says the Dominant, and with a quick thrust, violates Caleb's asshole.

"Oh, Jesus," he gasps into Holly's cunt as the head pops into him. The feel of his warm breath uttering that expression of dismay only drives Holly further into her hunger, and she twists her hand in his hair.

"Did I tell you to talk?" she growls, and grinds her pussy more firmly against his face.

"No, Mistress," comes Caleb's muffled grunt, and he begins tonguing her sex in earnest. The Dominant's cock slides deep into his ass, and an expression of utter joy crosses the woman's face as she meets Holly's eyes over the writhing curves of Caleb's back.

Holly normally only gets to come once when a man goes down on her; she's too polite to ask for more, though she almost always wants it. She feels a faint hint of nervousness at letting Caleb—no, *making* him—continue, a torrent of thoughts running through her head. *His tongue will get sore. His neck will get tired. I'm a whore for wanting so much.*

Then she pushes her crotch harder against Caleb's face, and his tongue wriggles into her with a fury.

She has never been eaten out like this. She has never felt such passion in the tip of a man's tongue, such excitement in its flat surfaces as they work her clit up and down. She has never been so sensitive when getting head, her clit engorged from her recent orgasm, her juices flowing freely onto the man's chin. She has never felt like she was going to come again so soon, right after coming the first time.

"The little fucker's hard again," said the Dominant.

Holly feels a swell of arousal. She grabs Caleb's hair, pulls his head back, and slaps him.

"Is this about your pleasure?" she growls. "Is this about your pleasure?"

"No, Mistress."

"Good," she snaps, and shoves his face back between her legs. Caleb's mouth works wonders now, every mounting second of his arousal making him service his mistress more eagerly. Holly begins to moan, unable to hold back her second orgasm any longer.

"Some guys come from getting ass-fucked," sighs the Dominant as she plows Caleb from behind, her hips pumping furiously against him. She's breathless from the exertion, her long brown hair no longer perfectly coiffed. "Think he's one of them?"

Perched on the curve of Caleb's ass, she reaches down

behind her and grabs his prick, gripping it hard and pulling on it so that he jerks and spasms.

Holly's eyes go wide; the Dominant does not jerk clients off. She does not jerk anybody off, Holly suspects. But Caleb is groaning and shivering like he's about to go off right now— to shoot his cum all over the floor.

She twists her hand in his hair and pulls his head back again. Another slap across his face, sending droplets of her juice in a fine mist into the close air of the dungeon. Another slap. A third.

"You think this is about your pleasure," she growls. "It's not about your pleasure at all, you selfish little prick. This is for me!" She almost screams the last sentence and slaps his face so hard he bleats: "Yes, Mistress! It's for you!"

Holly is so turned on by his evident distress that when she shoves his face back into place and feels his tongue seething against her clit, she realizes she's going to come. This time she doesn't care if she's the one to end the scene—and she doesn't care if Caleb comes or not, because she can see the Dominant's cock stretching his asshole in long stroking thrusts, coming out glistening with lube each time. It's the sight of that, and the sight of the Dominant's arm working viciously up and down to torment Caleb's cock and balls, that drives Holly over the edge.

She comes so hard this time that she sees stars, almost losing her balance on the chair. She would have tipped the god-damned thing over if she wasn't able to hook the toe of her boot under the spanking bench. Thank god the Dominant bolted it to the floor.

Her orgasm flashing white-hot through her, Holly gasps and finishes, the pleasure growing so intense she can't stand another instant. The tension in her body mounts as Caleb tongues her. Holly grabs his hair and pushes, tipping over the chair for real this time, leaping to her feet as she pulls her sex away from Caleb.

He looks up at her frightened—has he displeased her? Then, his face goes all twisted and raw, as the Dominant tugs on his balls harder.

"There's a wine glass in the kitchen cupboard," said the Dominant. "Go get it. He's going to shoot a lot."

Her legs quivering, Holly races into the kitchen and finds the cupboard with shaking hand. She can't find the wine glasses but grabs a goblet. When she returns, the Dominant has slid her cock out of Caleb's ass and is crouching down, stroking his cock.

"You can do the honors," she says. "I'll hold the glass."

Holly gives the Dominant the glass and wraps her hand around Caleb's cock. The Dominant lifts the glass so that his head is just below the rim. Can't miss a drop.

It only takes a few strokes, Holly's hand pumping streams of cum out of Caleb's prick. He groans as he comes for the second time. She knows from experience: The second one is almost always more intense. This one makes him gasp.

The Dominant reaches in to squeeze the last drops out of Caleb's softening cock. She withdraws the glass and holds it up for Holly.

Holly accepts it and comes around to Caleb's face.

Seating herself again, she tips his head back and brings the glass to his lips. There's not really much of it—a few milliliters, at best—but it's enough to flow from the bottom of the goblet between Caleb's obediently parted lips. He drinks his own cum, looking up at Holly in abject humiliation.

When it's as empty as it's going to get, Holly hands the Dominant the goblet. The Dominant bends forward and kisses her on the lips, this time open-mouthed. Their tongues intertwine, and the Dominant smiles.

"I'll give you a few minutes," she says, and takes the glass into the kitchen.

Holly caresses Caleb's face. They are at the end of their hour. Holly doesn't know what to say. *Thank you? Fuck you? I love you? I hate you?*

So Caleb says it: three words Holly's always hated to hear, especially from someone who just gave her something precious.

But this time she doesn't mind because she's been moved so completely by Caleb's surrender. The pain isn't the moving part; Caleb is not a masochist, but neither is he a wimp. He plays football, rock climbs, mountain bikes, reads legal briefs; pain's no big deal. Nor is the humiliation what moves her. Caleb is a very proud man, but he knows that all bedroom games stop at the door to the bedroom —or, in this case, the dungeon.

No, what moves Holly is that she couldn't do it— couldn't *have* done it, without his help. She's too nice a person to get what she wants. She's too nice a person, which is probably why she's dating a vanilla guy, a lawyer, former football player, former frat boy, mountain biker, fan of Bruce Willis movies, a guy who thinks missionary-position sex is plenty hot and would never dream of making an appointment with a professional Dominant, even if he does fit this one's "profile."

She's too nice a person to do what she's always wanted: tie up the man she loves and hurt him, torture him, humiliate him. Preferably—it was almost required—while he protested and begged her not to hurt him. She confessed her need to him, which was not that big a deal. He said "yes," which was a big deal. She still couldn't do it, which was the biggest deal of all, and a serious pain in the ass for about the last a year and a half.

And now she has done it, and here is Caleb, bloodied but unbowed, his cum-slick lips affectionately kissing her thighs and mouthing the words "I love you."

"I love you too," she says, the words feeling strange in her mouth—far, far stranger than any of the words she's spoken so far this evening. And then, she says something that felt far stranger in this context: "Thank you."

"Don't mention it," he says, his cocky frat-boy snarkiness showing through. She is frightened for a moment that he is going to say "Happy Valentine's Day," which will blow the whole thing and make her feel awkward. But he doesn't. He just adds, "Don't mention it, Mistress."

She doesn't laugh at that.

She feels the quiver in her stomach that always comes from doing something she shouldn't.

"You don't hate me?" she says, her voice small. "You don't think I'm a bad person?"

"Oh, please," he says.

Her eyes narrow.

"Mistress," adds Caleb quickly. "I don't think you're a bad person, Mistress."

Holly feels her stomach calming. "That's better," she sighs, and reaches out to retrieve her thong.

TAKING IT ALL

Rachel Kramer Bussel

Kim was amazed at how everything suddenly shifted as soon as she stuck the cock down her pants. She'd worn a strap-on before, but always during the context of sex, right before she was about to fuck someone, a hurried, heat-of-the-moment action intimately tied to sticking her dick into some girl's eager hole. That she could possess a cock without another girl around was a new and exciting thing for her, like any girl she saw could be the one to discover Kim's new secret. This time, she wore her cock proudly, letting its weight mark and change her. She'd always wondered what it'd be like to have a cock, and now she knew: She felt strong and powerful, capable of conquering heroic tasks along with bedding the hottest girls around, a boost to her natural inner confidence. She didn't analyze this feeling too much, simply took it for granted.

There was something macho about the toy, something manly that vibrators and other sex toys simply didn't offer. Mind you, Kim didn't look like a guy, with her jet-black hair, eyeliner circling her lids, slash of lipstick, safety-pin-laden black shirt, dark jeans, and huge black sneakers. She looked like a punk kid trying a little too hard to wear her toughness on her sleeve while also showing off her curvy bod. Her fuck-you flirtatiousness was designed to both attract and repel, and it seemed to work on both counts, sometimes a little too well, doing the former with the girls who were slightly too polished for her taste, the latter with the ones she wanted to get her hands on. But for all her firm beliefs and strictly defined parameters, Kim's taste sometimes surprised her. She'd see a girl and feel as if she couldn't do a single thing until she had her, absolutely and completely, no questions asked. She'd stop everything she was doing, thinking, feeling in order to pursue her quest. The cock only made her more feel this all the more.

When she surveyed the party, it was clear right away who'd be the lucky recipient of her cock; even before she knew her name, Kim knew she wanted to corrupt this perfect stranger. The girl looked as pert and cute and sweet as a flower, in a clingy paisley dress that stuck to her breasts, letting her hard nipples poke out. She had one leg crossed over the other, her smooth, pale legs shown off to perfection. Her gaze was a studied one of bored beauty, as though she was just waiting to be swept off her feet. When their eyes met, it only took a second for Kim to know she was the one, the one who would take Kim's cock's virginity, would complete the race Kim felt like she'd started. Wearing the cock was only half the battle, boosting her up into someone stronger and braver. But she'd know for sure once she slid it into a hot girl, and this girl, with the challenging look on her face and slowly rising skirt hem, was perfect, Kim decided. It was in part the cock talking, but it was also some long-buried part of Kim; her cock made her feel big and strong and powerful, larger than her smallish frame would make you think, as if by putting it on she'd become someone else, someone sexier, hornier, fiercer. She didn't want to quietly enjoy this secret pleasure, although she definitely did: the weight and bulk of it, hidden in her pants, the way a slight, subtle jiggle could send it pressing against her already-throbbing clit. She wanted to pull down her pants and show off her new equipment, slide her hand up and down the toy, own it as if she'd been born with it. And every time she looked at Sara, she wanted to grab her, corral her: in a word, *have* her.

Kim had fucked plenty of girls before, ravished them so that they screamed and tugged at her hair and raked their nails deep into her skin, but this was new. She'd never been so totally consumed by the desire to defile. She itched to stick her hands down her pants, play with her new toy, but she resisted. Had she taken a Viagra or something without even noticing? She felt like a horny guy, the kind who leers at every girl who passes by, who has a permanent erection he wants everyone to know about. Kim felt like this, and, for the first time, sympathized with the guys she knew who always gave her a hard time, begging to fuck her just once. But she wasn't going to beg; she'd make the other girl do the begging.

Kim sauntered over to the bar, ordering a soda as she bided

her time, waiting to be noticed. She had no doubt that she would; in their relatively small dyke scene, everyone noticed Kim at some point or another, but she'd carefully cultivated a persona that said mainly, "look but don't touch." Kim launched into a conversation with the bartender, nonsense chitchat she managed to become engrossed in so that she could forget about Sara for a minute. She had to block her out of her mind, as if physically moving a rock or heavy piece of machinery, in order to go about her evening.

Kim did such a good job that when Sara politely asked the bartender if she could smoke, the sound of her voice startled Kim. It might have anyway, since in their small town with an even smaller, more tight-knit dyke population, they'd never met. Or maybe this girl was new, but in either case, it felt to Kim like her cock, the one that was so new yet felt so old and familiar, this new/old part of her seemed to remember the girl's voice, the girl's curves, and as the girl shifted in her chair, Kim felt her cunt aching and would have sworn that her dick got harder in her pants. She glanced over, and because of the way Sara was leaning forward against the bar while the bartender took his time rustling up a match, her skirt had ridden up so it was about to expose her ass. As it was, the skirt clung tightly to the curves of Sara's behind, illuminating all Kim needed to know. All of a sudden Kim had a vision of Sara on her hands and knees, that perfect ass right in her line of sight as Kim slid the dildo in and out of her puckered little hole. It was so strong she might have called it a premonition, but she snapped back out of it when she saw Sara look at her. Kim reached for the smoke Sara held between her fingers, stuck it in her mouth, whipped out her lighter before the bartender could, lit it, took a puff, and slowly exhaled in Sara's face, then took it out, turned it around, and offered it up to Sara's startled lips.

"Should I thank you for that?" the girl asked with something like a sneer in her voice as she took a deep drag.

Kim stepped closer until they were practically touching, until the soft folds of Sara's skirt almost brushed against her beloved cock. "No, but you should thank me for the fuck of a lifetime you're gonna get as soon as you finish that cigarette. And, by the way, I'm Kim," she finished. As soon as the words were out, she couldn't believe she'd uttered them; just like drinking sometimes made her say surprising things, today the cock was serving the same function.

Sara stared back at her, clearly torn between continuing her defiance and the unbearable arousal that was slowly snaking its way down from her reddened face. Kim knew that they were drawing attention to themselves but didn't care; she knew most of the people in the room, and if Sara was overly bothered by their prying eyes, her lust seemed to overcome that uncertainty quickly enough. Sara threw the butt onto the ground, mashed it, uttered a quick, "Sara," and then grabbed Kim, kissing her almost angrily. But Kim had the upper hand and hoisted Sara by her waist over her shoulder. Sara squirmed but didn't actually do all that much to escape Kim's grasp, and she carried the girl out of the bar to the applause of everyone inside. Kim even heard a few shouts of "You go, girl!" and "Show her what she can do with that sweet ass" from the rowdier women in the crowd. She put her down a few steps out the door, and it was all she could do not to lift her skirt right there on the pavement. Kim's whole body was throbbing, begging her to get on with things already.

They walked silently, with Kim leading the way. Their silence spoke volumes as Kim strode purposefully, as if her cock were leading her along, while Sara strolled behind, giving off the occasional huff but not showing any inclination to go somewhere else. Kim wondered how guys managed with a real, live cock practically bursting out of their pants every day; she felt wild and out of control with this new appendage, as if every moment not spent fucking was a sad waste.

They reached the door, and as Kim fumbled with her key, Sara was the one who pressed up against her backside, rubbing one thin leg between Kim's legs, certainly feeling what lurked beneath. Kim's breath caught, but she simply reached behind her, tugging Sara inside until they finally reached her apartment door. The few minutes that had elapsed seemed agonizing, and Kim was going to make Sara pay for every second she'd had to wait.

Kim shoved Sara against the wall so the girl's face was right up against the spackled whiteness, leaving no room between her flushed cheeks and heaving breasts and the hard, unyielding surface. Kim smiled to herself when her date's hands automatically went over her head into that universally subservient sign. Kim reached under the short dress and pulled Sara's panties down, making sure Sara could feel the elastic digging into her slim thighs, could feel herself trapped in place. Then Kim pushed down her pants, unveiling the cock that had so quickly become a part of her. She slipped a tiny sample packet of lube from her pocket, pouring some over the dildo and some onto her fingers. With one hand, she reached around, stroking along Sara's wet cunt, and with the other she probed Sara's small, sweet asshole. Even her back door looked somehow demure, if such a thing were possible. The more pristine Sara appeared, the more Kim wanted to take her down, to defile her and make her roar in messy, loud, wild agony. When Kim's first two fingers slid into Sara's asshole, and her other hand traipsed along Sara's pussy lips and over her clit, the girl let out a noise, a cross between a yell and a strangled moan.

Kim knew it was time. "I've been waiting to get you right here ever since I laid eyes on you tonight. This perfect little ass of yours was staring right at me, and I'm about to fuck you so hard you'll remember me every time your ass so much as twitches." The words just seemed to come out of her, as naturally as her cock pushed into Sara's asshole, while they both struggled to contain themselves. Sara was already rocking back and forth, her hips taking on a rhythm that Kim couldn't help but follow as she watched the red cock disappear between Sara's cheeks. Kim was overcome with excitement, more so than she could ever remember; it was a kind of arousal that seemed to seep from her pores, fill her brain, sink down into her bloodstream and back out through her clit. The truth is, it had little to do with Sara herself, as hot a number as she was. Kim was mostly awed by the way her cock took on the qualities she most associated with butches: strength, power, self-assurance. Kim had always considered herself tough, but in a scrawny, scrappy, punkish underdog way; this cock gave her something else, something that allowed her to fuck a girl like Sara in the ass when it was almost guaranteed they weren't going to see each other again. That no longer mattered; nothing did, except the way the cock parted Sara's perfectly round hole, the way Kim could feel every wiggle Sara made, the way Kim slammed her hips up against Sara's, pinning her to the wall, as she bit her neck and admired the mark she left. Kim was taking everything Sara gave her, taking it all and then demanding more, pushing the girl until she cried out. Kim reached down and shoved two fingers into Sara's cunt, no longer awed at how juicy she found her. Kim thrust upward and in, then slowly slid out, admiring the shiny cock, wishing she had a camera to record this moment of triumphal emergence, of her dick's reigning dominion over Sara's ass.

Kim felt her body trembling as Sara wiggled against her, begging for more. Looking down at the inanimate toy she held in her hand, she felt something click inside her. As the base pressed back against her clit, it was like lighting a firecracker, its heat spreading up and into her body, about to set it off into an explosion, the likes of which she might never recover from. Kim felt tears well up in her eyes, tears of shock and joy that this toy she'd bought on a whim, this cock that looked nothing like her body, felt like much more than simply an object made in a factory that she'd purchased with the intention of getting herself, and other girls, off. This cock, made of glitter and red silicone and passion, felt special, as if by virtue of being pressed up so tightly against her skin it had become an extension of her true self. This was the first time Kim had worn one "just for fun," as her friend Lee had said. But Kim quickly found that it was more than just "fun." She'd gained what felt like magical powers that extended deeper than the farthest reaches of Sara's ass, to a place so deep inside she wasn't sure she'd ever visited it before.

Instead of an actual camera, though, Kim simply had her mind, that perfect recording device, which would set the moment on automatic replay for a long time to come. She pulled out, then teased Sara with the head of the cock, waiting until Sara begged before pushing it back in. "Please, Kim, fuck my ass, I need you, I need your cock—" she broke off when she got exactly what she was asking for. Kim closed her eyes and slammed into Sara's ass, focused solely on the way the cock pressed back against her clit, the way Sara's hips felt when she held them in her hands, and what she imagined the head of the cock looking like as it speared Sara's tightness again and again. Kim got lost in the sensation, the taking, overtaking, the claiming—not just of Sara's ass, but of a missing part of herself. She had no room left to ask Sara how it felt; she simply trusted that the cock was everything Sara had been looking for, too, as she thrust in and in and in until she couldn't go any deeper and just stayed buried there while her fingers pushed so far into Sara's pussy she could feel the cock through her slippery walls. Sara gave a garbled yell and tightened her grip on Kim's fingers, coming in a silent series of spasms that made Kim's clit leap as well. Kim stayed inside Sara's ass long after both their orgasms were over, too shaken to leave that safe embrace that had given her exactly what she'd needed.

She knew Sara was just a vessel, a tiny piece of a larger puzzle, but for now, she was all Kim had. They both stayed there, breathing heavily, for as long as they could, before the silence became too deafening. Everything after was hardly worth remembering. For Kim, it ended there, at that moment, her cock in Sara's ass, both girls lost in thought, utterly shaken by what they'd been through. In that lingering silence, they'd looked at each other, their gazes searching, but Kim was the first to break their eye lock. What she'd gained from fucking Sara had, in many ways, been about her own needs, her own wants. She pulled Sara close to her, a long, hard, silent hug that would just have to be enough. Sara didn't say a word, but when they walked out the door back into the night, she laced her hand through Kim's, squeezing it hard—by silent agreement, hello, goodbye, and thank you all wrapped up into one motion. They each knew they'd go their separate ways, and Kim knew that nothing would ever be the same for her again. Not surprisingly, she was right, and five years later, Kim still has the cock to prove it, though it still takes a special kind of girl to take all of it, and all of her.

POSTCARDS

Mike Kimera

Annette had promised herself she would not open the latest postcard until the evening, but she had woken to an arousal she couldn't ignore, so here she was, at the computer, searching for stimulation; something to light up her mind's eye while her fingers worked their magic on her demanding flesh. If things had been different, she might have searched the Web for fucktales to lubricate her lust or lurked in chat rooms where strangers would spew their fantasies over her. Instead she double-clicked on the folder that held the "postcards" from her husband.

Annette knew by heart the first postcard her husband had sent her, the one that had caught her by surprise, the one that had changed things between them. She smiled as she remembered how pleased she had been to receive an e-mail from him after only one night away from Chicago. She had opened it expecting his usual humorous observations on people and places. What she found made her catch her breath. It read:

In my mind last night, my cum was on your breasts, not my hands. You were kneeling. Your arms were tied behind you so that your palms met, as if in prayer, between your shoulder blades. Your breasts jutted outward until I caught them in my hands and squeezed them together, making a channel for my cock. The vibrator in your cunt was making you sweat as I oiled your breasts. The clamp on your clit made you gasp when I placed it there. Standing, leaning forward, pushing you back on your heels, I fucked the soft meat of your tits. My cum splashed your neck and chin and dripped slowly onto your breasts. Afterward, I watched you struggle to climax while my drying sperm puckered your skin.

He had never written to her like this before. Nor had he ever restrained her. From the immediate tightening of her cunt and the hardening of her nipples, she had realized it was something that she had wanted him to do but about which she had never spoken to him.

Sex had always been the heartbeat of Annette's marriage. The strong sex drive that had been hers since puberty was amplified by Olivier's presence until her lust for him became central to her life. She hungered for him, needed to feed from him daily. He was the cocaine to which her libido was addicted, yet their marriage was anything but harmonious. He was very French: passionate, verbal, fond of argument. She came from a long line of combative Irish New Yorkers. The two of them fought, they sulked, they embarrassed friends with the vitriol they would pour on each other's egos. But always they came back: their bodies forced into fiercely passionate struggles that ended with both of them exhausted and nothing resolved. Each day the tension would start anew, pulling at them, inflaming them, holding them together.

In the first three years of their marriage they had never once spent a night apart. Then the company started to ask Olivier to travel. He would be away for a week at a time, usually in a different time zone.

The first time it happened, the week had seemed to stretch forever. When he returned she fell upon him in a frenzy of need. That weekend was a blur of sweat and sex, but the fucking was too frantic to be satisfying. An anxiety had entered Annette's mind, marring her enjoyment. Olivier was an attractive man who needed the company of women and the release of sex. How many weeks could he live in hotel rooms without seeking solace in the arms of a stranger?

Before he left in the early hours of Monday morning, Olivier had woken Annette by placing his hand between her legs and kissing her still-closed eyes one at a time. She opened her legs but kept her eyes closed. Pushing his fingers gently into her he had whispered, "You are my desire. Remember that." Then he was gone, as fleeting and insubstantial as a dream.

The next night the first postcard had arrived. Annette knew that this was Olivier's way of staying focused on her. She imagined him in his hotel room, naked at his laptop, conjuring erotic images to stoke her desires and to prove his love.

Olivier returned late on Friday. Neither of them mentioned the postcard, but the sex that night had an extra edge. Olivier was strong and forceful, holding her hands above her head as he fucked her, each stroke driving her back into the mattress. She had worn a silk scarf around her neck that evening, not her usual style of dress, and had taken care to leave it by the bed. When he took her for the second time, Oliver used the scarf to bind her hands behind her back as she rode up and down on his cock, struggling to keep her balance. She did not resist, knowing she had invited this, wanted this. At the end Olivier grasped her breasts tightly, pulling her down onto him, forcing himself up into her. Her orgasm was intense. She collapsed forward onto him and fell asleep with her hands still tied.

Annette still had the scarf. She liked to keep it near her when Olivier was away. Sitting in front of her computer, the scarf wrapped around her wrist, she let her fingers slide over the smooth warmth of her inner thigh. On impulse she avoided the newest postcard and went instead to the second one she had received.

Olivier had been home in Chicago for two weeks and then had suddenly been called away. The day after he left, the second postcard arrived. It read:

I'm in Madrid thinking of you. A rope is between your legs. Unless you stay on tiptoe it rides up into your cunt. Your nipples are clamped. An elastic cord stretches from the clamps to bolts in the floor. If you stand on tiptoe your breasts are pulled and stretched. Your head is pulled all the way back. Your hair is gathered together and tied to a butt plug, lodged in

your ass, forcing you to arch your back. A lit candle is in your
mouth. You are waiting. For me. And my whip.

This image was harder for her to accept. Pain had never appealed to her, so the whip made her anxious. She had had anal sex, but never with Olivier, and although she owned a little blue vibrator to help her through the night, she had never pushed anything into her asshole. She tried to imagine Olivier tying her like that, wondering how she would seem to him, how it would feel to be so helpless.

The next day she made her first visit to a sex shop. Nervously she selected a butt plug and some lubricant. She went directly home, stripped, and pushed her new toy into place. She felt incredibly full. She knew it was already evening in Madrid. She phoned Olivier's hotel room.

"Olivier D'Or." His voiced sounded rich and strong.

"The butt plug is filling me," she said, needing to let him know immediately, not wanting a preamble.

Silence. Then the sound of a zipper being opened.

"I'm pretending it's your fat cock forcing its way inside me."

She could hear him stroking himself but he said not a word.

"It hurts. It hurts so good. I want you to take me. And take me again. To stretch me. I want to feel your seed shoot inside me. Fuck me, you bastard. Fuck me hard. Use me."

Leaning back on the bed, the phone trapped against her neck, she reached for the little blue vibrator.

"I'm pushing my vibrator into the base of the butt plug. God it feels good."

Olivier was breathing hard now. She pictured him jacking off in his hotel room, listening to her playing the whore.

The vibrator made her shiver from the base of the spine up. She forgot about painting verbal pictures for Olivier and focused on her own needs, working her clit with her free hand.

She heard the familiar sound of Olivier coming as she thrashed on the bed, then she let her own orgasm possess her.

When she was still, she put the receiver to her ear again and said, "If you were here now, I would lick you clean and suck you until I could have you again. I need you. Come home soon." Then she put the receiver back in the cradle and ended the call.

Olivier didn't contact her for three days, long enough for Annette to think about the phone call time and again. Sometimes she would be convinced that she had gone too far and Olivier thought she had slipped into a sexual dementia. At other times she'd work herself up into anger: He should be grateful to her, she'd decide; men paid good money to get that kind of call.

Once Olivier was in front of her again, though, her strongest emotion was lust. Even after a long-haul flight, he moved as if he owned the world. People parted before him like a shoal of minnows in the path of a shark. Her cunt ached at the sight. She had decided to meet him at O'Hare. She had intended to slap him for not calling her. Now all she wanted to do was fuck.

Olivier's face changed completely when he saw her. The stay-the-fuck-out-of-my-way look that his face habitually wore when he traveled was transformed for a second into joy before he recovered himself and tried to look severe.

When he reached her, he gathered her in his arms and lifted her off the floor. When their kiss ended, she said, "Why didn't you call?"

Olivier smiled and whispered in her ear, "I wanted to keep fresh the memory of your fucked ass."

His left hand had found its way to Annette's buttocks as he talked. He used it to push her up against his erection as he said, "I haven't let myself come in three days."

Annette felt his strong fingers pushing against her asshole through the fabric of her summer dress and struggled in that too public place, but Olivier held her in position.

"Tonight I will stretch your asshole with my cock until I hear you scream and beg for more," he promised.

Now, as she sat in front of her computer, her fingers moving lightly over her labia, Annette remembered that night, the first night that he had sodomized her, and smiled. It was as if that was when her marriage had really begun, when he had finally made her his.

She could smell her own sex now. Her nipples were starting to ache. It was time to open Olivier's latest postcard. With two fingers pushing into her cunt, she read:

In the mirror in front of you, you can see how distended your breasts look, pulled straight out by the clothespins on your nipples, which are fastened to the base of the mirror by elastic ties at full stretch. The bright blue ball gag keeps your mouth open so wide that your jaw aches. Saliva runs from each side of your mouth. Your hands, wrists, and elbows are tied closely together and stretched above your head so that, were your ankles not tied to the chair, you would barely be able to stay on the seat.

The "seat" is a birthing stool, designed to keep your legs apart. Aimed at your clit is a high-pressure hose. At random intervals and for random lengths of time, it punches water at your clit. Sometimes hot. Sometimes ice cold. I have told you I will be back in an hour. There are still five minutes to go. So far you have come twice.

Annette groaned and bit her lip. How did he do this? How did he know the secret images that would consume her with lust? She read on:

I enter the room early and switch off the water. I am carrying a whip made out of small lengths of hosepipe. The handle is shaped like a cock. You know it fits, just, in your ass.

I kiss you on the forehead and whisper, "let's see your breasts change color."

The hoses are only eighteen inches long but there are four of them. At the end of each hose is a plastic bead. You know that the beads leave angry red depressions in your skin. Holes have been punched into the beads so that they whistle as they move through the air toward your flesh. The beads bite where they touch, and a line of fire traces back from those bites across the tender surface of your breasts.

At first you cannot believe the pain. You scream into the gag, desperate for me to stop. Then the rhythm takes you. You become the pulsing points of pain. You stiffen when you hear the beads move through the air and shudder when they hit. You thrash and moan and stare in disbelief at the marks that have trans-formed your breasts.

You look relieved when I go to unclamp your crushed nipples and then scream into your gag once more when the blood rushes back into your abused flesh.

While you are still screaming I force the whip handle up into your cunt, then I stand behind you, wrapping my cock in the soft strength of your hair, pushing myself through it, brush-ing against your cheek, until my cum splashes over your face and up into your hair.

Annette was panting now. The images were so raw and so violent that they frightened her. Despite that, she felt her cunt contract around her fingers and coat them with her spend.

In the warm afterglow of her orgasm, Annette knew that Olivier would never hurt her so badly in reality, but she hoped that he would return home on Friday with a bright blue ball gag ready for her to try.

HOW WE PLAY

Debra Hyde

I kneel before Carl, wondering what the hell he wants. I'm blindfolded, hands cuffed behind my back, and I'm in my nightgown. Carl's at the kitchen table sipping his coffee and reading the morning paper. I can hear the paper rustle, him sipping. His laughter tells me he's on the editorial page, reading cartoons.

And he's not saying a word to me. He's not paying any attention to me.

This is freaky. I'm always naked and getting toyed when he ties me up. Why the clothes? And why is Carl ignoring me?

Naked, I could entice him with a flash of pussy but dressed I can't. I can't be anything more than an ornament so I sit there like some discarded toy.

Carl puts down the paper, gets up, and pours himself another cup of coffee. I hear him spooning sugar into his cup and stirring its contents. I hear the spoon clatter against saucer, metal to china.

It would be all so quaintly domestic if not for my questionable position, but before I can ask Carl, I hear shouting at our front door—shouting and bodies bursting through the door. A foyer vase crashing to the floor, a rush of feet. Hands grabbing for me.

It happens so fast I can't even yell for Carl. I can only scream as I'm lifted up. Duct tape slapped across my mouth shuts me up, and then I hear Carl laughing.

"Tell them she needs the fight taken out of her."

I'm hauled from the house like a worn-out upholstered chair on big-item trash day. I'm carried down the front steps to the driveway, where I'm unceremoniously dumped into the backseat of a vehicle.

Captors, I have captors, and they know I can't break my fall with my hands behind my back. They check me for neck and shoulder injury. They know what they're doing—they're experienced.

Trouble is, I'm not.

The door slams shut, but instead of climbing into the front of the vehicle, one of my captors speaks, apparently at the driver's window. "She's okay with the tape, breathing fine. She's all yours." Another voice adds, "He said to tell you that she needs the fight taken out of her." A hand pounds the hood of the vehicle, signaling our send-off.

Carl's arranged this abduction. Apparently a friend of a kinky friend of a kinky friend goes a long way. I have no idea who has me, and it's thrilling.

That's when I smell it: cinnamon, wafting through the air. Soothing, warm cinnamon.

Now I know. I know who has me and, damn, if I don't want to kiss Carl for it.

They're rough with me as we climb the stairs, Marce leading the way and Scot pushing me from behind. Dykes to die for, one has me by the arm while the other prods me with the flat of her hand between my shoulder blades.

"Hustle. Move that girly ass of yours."

I stumble, trying to comply with Scot's butch demands, but I can only move as fast as Marce lets me, and she's not exactly rushing to the front door. It's a no-win situation, a catch-22 meant to create a quandary. I don't know what to do, but then, I've never done this before.

The door gives way and, together, Scot and Marce drag me into the foyer. Stumbling, I'm a clumsy oaf wedged between them, lacking all grace. It's fucking embarrassing.

Marce pulls me forward then pushes me up against the wall. She presses into me, puts her hand to my throat and rips the tape from my mouth. It stings, but before I can cry out, she crushes me with a rough kiss. I have no idea where any of this is going, but it's starting off just right.

Marce's tongue is insistent, and her mouth is wide and wet, but mine's gone dry from shock and suspense. She pulls the blindfold from my face, but I'm so overwhelmed by her kiss that I can't bear to keep my eyes open. She smells lightly of jasmine and aloe vera, but these feminine scents are countered by her rough hands, one at my throat, the other at my tit, squeezing and caressing. I feel small and pliant in her sure grip.

Nearby, Scot laughs, and I feel strangely disembodied. I can't help it; I've wanted to play with Scot and Marce forever and now that I'm in their clutches, girl that I am, I'm an easy mark.

But this is how we'll play: rough, sexual, top and bottom clearly defined but wrestlers all the same. First they wrest me from my usual surroundings, then I'll wrestle against what they do to me. I'll struggle through whatever sensations they'll foist upon me.

Marce barely concludes her kiss when Scot grabs me by the hair and drags me from her embrace. I'm surprised how vice-like the human hand can be—surprisingly immobilizing. My head twists in whatever direction that's convenient to Scot, and I can't help but stumble yet again.

I'm hauled before an arm mitt dangling from a hoisted ceiling chain. Marce spins me around and frees me from Carl's cuffs. Scot grabs my wrists and shoves my arms into the mitt. She laces it tight and secure, leaving me held in its grip, and before I can get used to it, Marce fusses something over my head—a hood!

It doesn't go on easily. Marce has to tug it into place, over my ears and nose, and the smell of leather engulfs me. As she laces the hood, it pulls my face tight and presses against my cheekbones, the bridge of my nose. It even stretches the corners of my eyes. I had no idea a hood felt this way.

Holes for my nose and mouth allow me some small mercy, but Marce attaches a blindfold to the hood, robbing me of sight.

A ceiling hoist cranks like an old wooden roller coaster, and my arms stretch upward. I guess I'm headed for the first hill of a different kind of drama, but where a coaster starts with a plunge, my drama starts with dangling. I'm stretched just enough to stress my shoulders, just enough to put me on my tippy toes. I get the distinct impression that the harder I squirm, the more likely I'll strain something. But I'm also poised to discover what comes next.

"God, you look ridiculous, hanging there in that night-gown," Scot teases. "It makes a muumuu look like haute couture."

"Ridiculous? She looks hideous! It's going to give me nightmares."

"It needs to come off."

A knife slides between fabric and flesh, and I hold my breath against it. Its edge tugs against fabric and pulls hard until it rips, first at one shoulder, then the other. The blade avoids my flesh. Its purpose is not to threaten me but to denude me, though by the time the ruined nightgown falls from me, I'm panting from its drama. I shiver from the excitement, and goose bumps break out on my body.

"Now you look good," Scot tells me. "Just like the slut we want to fuck."

Scot's at my ear, speaking lewdly. Her cinnamon wafts in the air, mingling with leather, and, delicious, it lulls me. Then, she strikes. She sinks her teeth into my neck. Pain shoots through my neck, wicked and sweet and all too brief.

"That's what you are, isn't it?" she asks, pulling away from me.

"Yes, Scot, that's what I am."

"What are you, girl?"

"A slut—your slut."

I'm at once humiliated and excited to admit it.

"Yeah, our straight-girl slut."

Lust knows no boundaries, I want to tell her, but it's too smart a claim for the gutter we're playing in.

Marce runs her hand down my spine. I'm uncharted territory to her touch, I want her everywhere, but I'm so new to this that even her finger trailing along my rump makes me shiver. She nears the wellspring of my lust, and I moan. When she slips a finger into me from behind, my cunt reveals a truth I wanted to hide.

"You're wet," she declares, pulling her finger from me. "Guess that says everything."

Indeed, it does, but I say nothing. Words need not endorse the obvious.

Their hands seize me and, like a splendid many-armed goddess, Marce and Scot maul me. Scot's laughter tells me that my despotic captors know exactly what they're doing.

This, too, is how we play. With words like slut, cunt, and bitch. With hands and teeth, groping and biting. With one body squirming against two, it ready to yield while the others wait to take. And it's more amazing than I ever imagined.

Scot's knife lies flat against my neck, its blade cold, stiff, and unforgiving. Like prey before the playful cat, I quiver against it. Its tip rises on point, posed to dance across my skin. I gulp against its tempered steel, which only seems to presses it deeper. It begins to wander, traipsing like a cat's claw down my neck, my sternum, to the fullness of my breast, scratching and tickling and confusing me. I can't tell whether it hurts or tickles as it circles one breast, then the other, swirling across my skin. Scot torments me with mixed messages of sensation as I dangle between screaming and giggling. It's like being held down, stung and tickled to death.

Finally, the knife's point comes to rest on my nipple. I stiffen and try to hold still against its implied threat. Again it strikes, this time pricking. Scot flicks her wrist rhythmically, causing a confusion of sensations and reactions—pain, shock, surprise—all so overwhelming that I feel like I'm choking against it. She stops only when she's pricked the entire circumference of my nipple, leaving it scraped and burning. I'm left gasping for breath and amazed.

I ache for the knife's hilt. I want it between my legs, its butt to my clit. *Put it there,* my moans convey. *Rub me there.* I spread my legs and offer myself as best I can in my hoisted position.

"Look at that. Straight girl wants to get fucked."

"Well, she's gonna have to wait."

It's Marce who observes and Scot who denies, and, denied, I whimper. But my whimpers change to moans when Scot makes good my one hope: She rests the butt of the knife against my clit. It rubs against me, against that sweet spot that responds to things cruel and wonderful. Fingers probe me from behind and spread within me. Marce tests my wet, cushioned interior.

God, yes, I want this. I want the pressing knife and probing fingers, and I'm surprised to feel myself ready to come. It

sprouts from the pressure of the knife butt and spirals outward, unfurling through my tunneled secret, wrapping itself
around Marce's fingers. Scot and Marce see me stiffen in reac-
tion, they hear me moan, and knife and fingers double-time
me, coaxing, urging, and pulling me toward that which they
want to exact from me.

I'm primed to deliver it and I don't disappoint them.
Suddenly, that keen spot explodes, and massive throbs course
through me, grabbing at Marce and forcing me to twist in my
bondage, to cry out, once, twice, then a third time. Again I'm
left panting, this time as the cascading thrill fades away.

"Nice," Scot comments. "Nice." Her voice is lascivious,
appreciative.

"She comes easily," Marce says. "And hard. My fingers are
cramped."

"Greedy cunt," Scot declares.

It's one thing when my dyke friends seize me, but when
my own body joins the plundering, I'm left breathless and
bewildered. Orgasm leaves me stupid with delight.

If orgasm leaves me stupid, it makes Marce and Scot down-
right horny. Dangling, I hear loud, wet kisses and can't help
but think that had they been a straight couple, I would have
thought "sloppy." But their kisses don't have that effect on
me. I'm too thrilled that they're going to fuck each other while
I dangle nearby.

"She makes me fucking hot," Scot says. "I need relief."

"Gimme," Marce answers.

They back up against the wall. A belt buckle loosens, and pants shimmy.

"Oh, baby, you're so wet."

Marce muffles then; only Scot makes intelligible sounds.

"Yeah, that's it. Right there, yeah."

I can only imagine how they look, Marce on her knees with her mouth busy at Scot's bush, tonguing Scot's lips there, teasing her clit and sinking into her hole.

"Take your shirt off," Scot demands.

Clothing rustles, and Marce's moans rise muffled but unmistakable.

"Yeah, on my clit," Scot directs. "Fingers, inside."

Now Scot moans.

"Yeah. Yeah. Give it to me."

Marce's noise tells me that Scot's playing with her tits as she caters to Scot's cunt. I'm surprised it's so much like a straight blow job.

Listening makes me want to watch. Like long ago when my double date ended up at a lovers' lane, a furtive evening born of dinner and a movie. They had the front seat; we had the back. They were slurped wet and sloppy; we were noisy. Everybody fucked and came and then fucked again with only slight glances at each other. I wanted to watch, but my date whispered "rude" in my ear. Still, I snuck peeks when he went down on me.

Listening brings out the voyeur in me. Scot's grunting now, and Marce is squealing. I bet she'll come away from Scot with her nipples pinched big and hard, looking like rough sex's aftermath.

Scot comes with a growl, predatory and fierce. She sounds like a guy. God, but I want to go down on her. Hell, I want to go down on anything.

"Your turn, baby," Scot tells Marce. "On the couch."

In the few steps to their couch, clothes fall by the wayside. The couch groans as they lie down, and I discover that Scot's the wet, sloppy one. She slurps over Marce's nipples.

Sounds of pleasure come from both of them. Scot loves Marce's breasts, Marce gets off on how Scot handles them, and Scot gets off on Marce's reactions. It's a perfect loop, and I want in on it.

I groan, long and low. I can't help myself, I feel so denied. Laughter from the couch.

"Think we should let her in on this?" Scot teases.

"Fuck yeah. She can eat me."

"Wonder how much sweet pussy she's had."

I haven't the balls to tell them not nearly enough.

Scot lowers me to standing and helps me guide my arms down from overhead. They're stiff, almost pins and needles, and I'm not sure I can balance myself without her.

But I'm not given time to adjust. Scot sticks a hand between my legs and laughs when she sees how wet I am. I barely have time to blush before she grabs me by the o-ring at the neck of the hood and hauls me over to the couch.

"Kneel, bitch. Let's see how long it takes you to find some pussy."

Marce's giggle tells me where she is and, groping along the couch's edge, I find her legs. While I kiss and lick my way along her legs, Scot returns to the couch and Marce's tits.

Suckling sounds and moans hasten me along my path, and soon I'm at the soft, delicious flesh of Marce's inner thigh, closing in on my goal.

I can smell Marce's nearness. It's light and sweet compared to Scot's more musky scent and I can't wait to close in on her clit. Her slit meets my tongue and, gasping, I slide my tongue upward, eager and ready for contact.

But a quick, startling slap to my nose rebuffs me. Scot's there, her fingers already working Marce's clit.

"In her hole, bitch. Fuck her in her hole."

Her mouth at Marce's tit, she mutters, "I get her clit" before her sloppy sucking resumes.

Nose burning enough to force tears, I whimper and tongue my way into Marce. There, lips part like curtains and beckon me onstage.

Warm, cushioned flesh envelops my tongue. I can't tell where her wetness begins and mine ends, and it doesn't matter as long as they linger together. Slowly, I move my tongue all around her, sensing and savoring every fold of flesh inside her. God, Marce is succulent. I want to stay like this forever.

But a hand grabs the top of my hooded head and pulls me away.

"I said to *fuck* her hole."

I'm slammed back into Marce's cunt and shown how to do it. My face is forced to fuck her, my stiff tongue a piledriver. When I react with a gasping moan, I'm let go.

"Don't stop, cunt, until after she comes."

My tongue, Scot's fingers, Scot's mouth: We use these things to make Marce come. I feel Scot masturbating her and match my rhythm to hers. Marce gyrates against my face, arches to Scot's finger as if she's rising to orgasm. It's breathtaking, and I'm so glad I moaned.

Finally, she comes. She thrashes against me and squeaks out a series of high-pitched squeals. Scot growls again, this time as conquering hero, and as I keep tonguing, a miracle flows around me, making my hooded face glisten wet. It's sweet like nectar and plentiful, and I drink it up.

Hearing me suck, Scot jokes, "No wet spot on the couch today!"

Finally, I let my tongue rest inside Marce. There, throbs ebb away, and I'm amazed to feel them against my tongue. Incredible. Absolutely incredible.

I'm left on my hands and knees, doggy style, waiting. I have no idea what comes next and the anticipation keeps me spellbound. I imagine their hands at me, one set grabbing me roughly by the nipples, pinching and pulling, while other hands tug at my labia. I imagine mouths sucking while hands plumb. I dream about that many-armed goddess capable of creating a tug of war that's at once both painful and delicious. Enthralled, I'm slack-jawed at my own thoughts.

Give it to me, I crave and beg. *Oh God, give it to me.*

Miraculously, a sudden sting answers my perverted prayer—Marce, pinching and pulling my nipple, stretching my tit out as far as it can go. Then, cruel slaps to the fullness of my breast. It smarts and it's exquisite.

"You like this, don't you?" she asks, her hand punctuating her declarations. "You're a slut for this."

She twists my nipple. I cry out.

"Aren't you?"

Another slap, then she switches to my other tit, stretching its flesh taut for her swats. I can't believe how good her tortures feel.

"Cunt. Say it. Cunt."

I moan and whimper. I'm too dumb with lust to answer her.

Another slap.

"Say it, bitch."

Words clog my throat. I can barely speak but somehow I spill the truth.

"Cunt," I utter. "I'm a cunt."

"For this," Marce commands.

"For this," I confirm.

Though brief and benign, the interrogation makes me ache. I want to get fucked and I want to come. As Marce tweaks and twists my nipples, Scot falls to her knees behind me, one hand resting on my ass.

Her other hand presses up flat against my vulva, aimed at my slit, my clit, and palm to slit, she spanks me. Scot is swift, her hand a hummingbird flitting at my flower, taking from me what she wants.

Scot doesn't make me say things. She doesn't make me admit my weaknesses. She just wants them dramatized, and in no time I'm arching and squealing. I explode against Scot's hand and reel from one of the biggest orgasms I've ever felt.

Pain made it that good. Relieved, I try to gasp my thanks. But my open mouth simply invites more opportunity.

Something firm and round pries into my mouth, something thick, short, and compact. It smells plastic and its taste is almost bitter, and I can barely open my mouth wide enough, thanks to the limiting hood. I reached out to brace myself for sucking and find it's strapped to thighs slick with sweet, fragrant juice. Marce, it's Marce, packing.

Another dick takes me from behind. It fights its way into me, pushing past my labia, pressing my hole to welcome its intrusion. It enters me, thick and long, the kind of cock I'd gag on if it shoved itself down my throat. I flinch as a meaty thumb forces its way into my ass and presses downward.

"Oh, God," Scot groans, "I can feel my cock in her."

Scot and Marce are in their own heaven, one that breaks the boundaries of their own lives, one that lets them throw off the social mores of same-sex pleasantries. They can do to me what's impolite and impolitic elsewhere—gangbanging like men in a porn scene where cocks capture holes, front and back, where they have a receptacle for their driving needs.

They're rough fucks, Marce and Scot. Marce pistons my mouth, keen on seeing how hard and fast she can fuck. Scot reams me, her dick a dowsing rod to my liquid, dipping and exploring before churning what it finds. Then, bored, she matches Marce's pace. Gripping me, hands front and back, pummeling me, cocks front and back, they bring me to a crying orgasm, the kind that's so good, it hurts.

As my throbbing cunt washes her beastly dick with slippery evidence, Scot lets out a "Damn, I love this straight girl!"

Marce laughs and pushes herself all the way into my mouth, teasing my gag reflex.

That's when I think of Carl, he who handed me over to

them—he who understands the expediency of giving his strange, straight girl over to her dyke friends for some extreme Sapphic sex. He'll bend me over the arm of his upholstered chair when I get home and he'll shove his cock into me. He'll order me to describe, detail by lurid detail, what Scot and Marce did to me, and he'll ream my ass with his thumb to make me squirm. And when I hit the right spot in my vicarious tale, Carl will pound me hard and give to me what Scot and Marce can't: He'll spew hot, wet spunk into me.

I think about sucking clean his flaccid cock and, as I do, cocks pull out of me, Scot's with a slurp. They void me, leave me empty and abandoned, lost with a tired jaw, a raw tongue, and a gaping wet cunt.

They're done with me, and I hope they're pleased and satisfied with me. I pray they'll want me back. But with thoughts of Carl's cum and my juice on my tongue, of his fluids leaking from me and running down my leg, I'm ready to go home. I'm ready for them to send me back.

Only they're not. I gag on a cock that tastes of cunt, while my ass protests against a protrusion larger than a thumb. But I accept both. I give myself over, ass and mouth to even more fucking. I sink into yet another rough delight. This, too, is how we play.

JUST TELL ME THE RULES

Cecilia Tan

"Just tell me the rules, Lila, just tell me the rules." Those were his words, the words that would change everything.

Or maybe it was my answer that changed things. Or maybe things had already changed, and I was too deep in denial to realize it. That's the most likely scenario, of course, given what had already happened, what we'd already done. I'll tell you how it went, and you decide.

Connor arrived the day after Jim went to Venezuela for two weeks hoping to close an oil deal. It had been one of those "old college friend needs a place to stay" kinds of things, and, it being Jim's apartment, I couldn't really say no. Still, the guy was supposed to come the day before so Jim could introduce us. But Connor's flight from Nairobi was delayed by a day because of a terrorism scare, so it was some hours after Jim's limo had left for the airport that a bedraggled and hollow-eyed man I'd never seen before showed up on the doorstep.

"You must be Lila," he said after I undid the deadbolt. He had a trace of British in his accent, along with other things. "Did I miss 'King James?'"

"You did," I told him as we wrestled his duffle bag into the foyer. The brownstone's entry was narrow, and there were two sets of doors to navigate before the stuff came to rest in the front hall. I opened my mouth to play hostess, offer him a cup of coffee or show him to his room or something, but he spoke first, as he sprang to the huge old mirror on the wall.

"This is lovely," he said, examining the wood with his nose mere inches from it. He ran his hand along the carved, curved lines of the frame. "Was it here when you moved in?"

I shook my head. "Estate sale. Jim loves antiquing."

"Jim, yes," he said not really listening to me, as he appraised the mirror, thoroughly absorbed by it. He had a shock of uncombed black curls hanging half into his eyes, which he didn't seem to notice. Then he turned to me and said, "So Jim hasn't told me much about you. Are you a world traveler, too, then?"

I stammered for a moment, not sure how to answer the question, not even sure what the question really was, and he went on.

"But where are my manners? Thank you so much for putting me up." His hand opened toward me and I instinctively took it. I found both of his, warm and dry, wrapped around mine in a way that was odd. It seemed completely natural to him but so foreign to me, so Old World, I suppose. I half expected him to kiss the back of my hand then, but he released me, that fully absorbed gaze now appraising my face. "Part Asian, are you then?"

"Uh, yes. Chinese, Filipina, Italian, Irish," I said. "In other words, American."

He laughed at that, a rich laugh like I delighted him beyond measure. "And so very San Francisco, as well," he said.

"Yeah, I guess," I agreed without really thinking about what he had said. "I thought Jim said you hadn't been to San Francisco before?"

"Oh, not for a long stay. I don't know my way around. But I have passed through once or twice. I get the sense of places very quickly. When you've lived as many places as I have, it's something you learn to do." Still that almost-stare, which would have seemed rude except there was some kind of enthusiasm behind it, some kindness. He was hard to read. "I'm looking forward to exploring the city a bit this time around, though . . ." he trailed off with a half smile.

"Let me show you your room," I finally said, wondering how we had spent so long standing there over his luggage.

It was something I would wonder about often the next few days, as it seemed like every time I talked to Connor about anything, we would wander onto a digression that would circumnavigate the earth before returning to the topic at hand, whether that was where to eat or which bus he should take to visit a museum. The fact that I couldn't read his signals, wasn't quite sure if we were on the same wavelength, only made him more intriguing to me. He was British by blood but had lived in India, Morocco, France. The irony was not lost on me that, white as he was, he would always be far more exotic than I was. I wanted to talk more and more with him, wanted to crack the code of his way of speaking, until the next thing I knew I went to the museum with him, went to eat with him. He assured me he could and would find his way around without trouble, but there I was, spending every waking moment with him. On the third day I realized the only times I'd ever been so engaged by a man had been when I was falling in love.

This realization came to me as we sat lingering over a bottle of wine at dinner at the little Italian place around the corner from the house. And Connor said to me, "So are we much alike, Jim and I, you think?"

I nodded. They were both forceful personalities, both energetic. "Only Jim is more . . . American. He travels the world, but he doesn't let as much of it rub off on him."

"Tell me what you mean by that." He twirled the red in the glass, the beginnings of a smirk in his eyes. Jim had told me they met in college, while both were traveling abroad. Now Jim traveled for work, as an international development officer for a multinational corporation, looking at oil, resources, economic development, a lot of stuff I didn't really care to think too deeply about. Connor, on the other hand, seemed to travel for the sake of travel, no fixed address, no fixed course in life, yet.

"Jim may be worldly," I said, "but you are of the world."

"And you, m'dear? What does that make you?"

I blushed and didn't know why. Wine and the late hour and a rakish man teasing me, that's why.

"You are the World," he declaimed.

"Tell me what you mean by that," I said, trying to mimic his tone—so interested, so intrigued. So easy to do.

"Child of Empire," he said, still full of poetry. "The story of colonization, cross-pollination, the strength of diversity." Then he snorted, deflating his own lofty balloon and switching gears, digressing. "What do you want to do with your life?"

I gave the automatic shrug. "I'm really at loose ends right now," I said. I had pursued a career in radio for a short while, then thought better of it. For the past six months, it had just been Jim and me. "I'm not really cut out to be a housewife, though."

He gave me a look that I read as "of course not" as he said, "So what is your arrangement with Jim?"

"You mean, domestically?"

He shrugged this time.

"Well, he is paying for everything right now. Until I find something else to do with my life. Maybe graduate school . . ." I broke off, as his appraising look had returned.

"Do you think you're going to marry him?"

If he had asked me a few months ago, I would have said yes. But by now the answer was "I might." Our parents were starting to act like they expected it, but there were "buts" beginning to form in my mind. Here I reached for his hand, because I was about to say something intimate. "I've been saving myself, you know."

"No!" he said, scandalized.

"Just in case." When three of your four grandparents are devout Catholics, it can have an effect. I had made out with boys at summer camp, dated a little in college, but the temptation to cross the line had never really been there. If I had met the right one, maybe. But I hadn't. Then. My heart seemed to hammer in my throat. "That must seem so backward to you."

"*Au contraire*. I find it fascinating." He squeezed my fingers in his, just a moment of warm pressure sending signals through my skin.

I became suddenly aware of how we must look to the waiter hovering off to one side, to the other few tables of people still in the place. Holding hands over a bottle of wine in the candlelight. I opened my mouth to say something nice about Jim, when I realized it might not come out sounding so nice. The guys I had dated before always reached a point where they wanted to push, and I would push them away. One of the nice things about Jim was that he didn't pressure me. What wasn't nice was the thought that flitted through my head: Was that why I'd stayed with him as long as I had? I wasn't about to get into a debate with myself over whether I loved him or not, not with Connor sitting there. I said something else to cover my thoughts. "You must be wondering how I got to be twenty-four years old without giving it up."

"No, actually, I was wondering how Jim has survived the past six months of living with you." His thumb paced softly up and down the edge of my palm.

"He's on the road a lot," I said, my voice neutral. "You know him."

"Lila," he almost a whispered it, "are you telling me you . . ." he paused, hunting for the right words, changing his tone from scandalized to sober. "Do you think he cheats on you?"

"Can it really be cheating if we're not married and we're not having sex anyway?" Connor didn't need to know those were Jim's exact words when I confronted him about the condoms I found in his toiletry kit. The same conversation in which he told me he would stop, that he would save himself for me, only for me, if I would marry him. My mind was so far in the past, going over those words, that I did not realize how they would sound in the present until I felt that thumb, rubbing my palm harder.

Suddenly I felt as if he were rubbing some other part of my skin. With his finger in motion, he seemed to wonder what it would be like to caress the curve of my shoulder, my breast. I shuddered as if he were doing it. "Jim," I said, my throat dry despite the wine, "doesn't consider it cheating."

"Where I come from," he replied, "it wouldn't be cheating either."

"Where do you come from?" I asked, trying to get the lightness back into my voice.

"The World," he said. "The World." And never said what 'it' was.

Back at the house I could barely make it up the stone steps to our front door, far more tipsy than the wine should have made me, but I felt giddy and frightened at the same time. This wasn't like sneaking out behind the bunkhouse with a boy who wanted to cop a feel but who'd blush to his roots if you called him on it. Connor was in charge, that much was obvious, while I tried to figure out exactly when it was I ceded control to him and what I'd agreed to.

Once inside, he carried me through the narrow hall to the room in back, the study we'd made into a guest room for him. He placed me on the futon couch, folded flat to make a bed, and began to peel me out of my clothes. I found it oddly reassuring that he kept his on, even as he bared me, sliding my panties down off my legs and then running his hands up my skin. I suppose I believed that as long as he had his pants on, I was safe. I could let him do as he pleased as long as he had his pants on. His nose followed the curve of my legs, and I felt his warm breath. He paused over the curly mound of my pubic hair, letting his warmth mingle with mine, before he pulled himself up to lie lengthwise beside me. I could feel the pulsing hardness of his erection through the fabric of his pants as it slid along my thigh. But I soon forgot it, as his fingers did what I had imagined, his warm, dry thumb circling my nipple, his mouth hot and wet on my neck as I arched into the sensation. He found those places on my neck that shoot pleasure down my skin, over my belly and into my crotch. He spooned me, one hand tipping my head back to keep my neck to his mouth, while the other hand slid over my skin, over the butte of my hip and down into the valley between my legs. His fingers picked up moisture there, rubbing slick between my still-closed lips. Then his leg crawled over mine, his foot, still in its sock, between my knees, pulling my top leg upward.

He opened me, and his fingers, held flat, skimmed the open space between my legs.

"God, Lila, so slick," he murmured in my ear, before returning his mouth to my neck.

He slid his hand back and forth slowly, increasing the pressure each time, spreading my lubrication around, until one finger separated itself from the others, seeking my clitoris, and finding it. I cried out. Jim and I had "petted" a few times in the past, but not like this. Before we had settled into our nice inertia of nonsexual stasis, he had tended to fumble, and had once, but only once, complained that he "didn't know what to do" if we weren't going to go all the way. Then he had stopped trying, which had suited my comfort zone. Connor seemed to know exactly what to do. His finger seesawed in time with the nerve impulses rippling from my neck over my skin. My hips began to buck and he squeezed me with his legs to keep me from writhing any harder against his hand.

"Can I put my finger inside you?" he asked. "Just one finger? Or would that be against the rules?"

The rules? It's hard to think when a man is touching you that way, when you're that close to orgasm. Other than not letting Jim (or anyone) put his dick inside me, I didn't know if there were other limits. There had not been the opportunities to test them. "I don't know . . ."

"What about your own finger? Can you put your own finger inside?" His sped up, fluttering against my clit like a thirsty dog's tongue. "Go on, Lila, put your own finger in."

I couldn't think of any reason why that should be verboten. I slipped my left hand around his, and let the tip of my middle finger partway into my vagina. My muscles contracted instantly, and he sped up yet faster.

"And how about orgasm—can you come, Lila? Would that be all right with you?"

My answer was nonverbal, as I shook in his arms, his legs, crying out without words. He lifted the pressure off my clit suddenly and my own hand was there, jamming my finger as deep as I could, as hard as I could, into myself. I rolled onto my stomach, my hips pumping into the bed, pumping myself onto my hand as the second wave of orgasm came over me and left me screaming, then gasping, face down on the comforter.

When I looked up, he was there, his head propped up on one elbow, watching me.

I said what one is supposed to at times like that. "What are you thinking?"

"I'm thinking that the man who takes your virginity is going to be one lucky bastard." He then reached down and pulled the extra blanket from the foot of the bed up over me, then excused himself to the toilet.

I lay there wondering what was going to happen next. More specifically, what would he do next? Was it his turn? I had been down this road with other men, and this was usually the time when they would ask for something in return. If I wouldn't do intercourse, what would I do? I was thinking over what I would consider doing when he returned, still zipping himself up as he came into the room, and said, "I won't object if you want to sleep down here with me, but

I won't be hurt if you want to go up to your own bed."

I was so confused by the fact that he wasn't now asking me to jerk him off or give him a blow job that I went to my own bed without questioning it. I replayed what had just happened in my mind again and again. Had I put a wall between us by saying he couldn't put his finger inside me? Did that imply more than I thought it did? I thought about the feel of his erection inside his pants, the hardness of it through the fabric, and the thought made everything at the core of me jump.

It was hours before I got to sleep, and then I woke up early, the sunlight filtering low through the blinds.

I tiptoed downstairs with this idea in my head that I just wanted to see him asleep. Like I was just going to look at him sleeping and then go back to bed. But I went buck naked, and after taking a moment to stare at him sleeping, I slipped under the covers next to him. I ran my hands along his chest, feeling my fingers part the hairs there, thinning out over his smooth stomach, and then sliding irresistibly lower. He slept in the buff and was already erect, breathing deeply, as I wrapped myself around him, one of my legs over his, my hand stroking him lightly. In my hand, he felt wrapped in an extra layer of silk compared to Jim.

He turned toward me, still asleep, a moan trapped in the back of his throat. His hands found my hips and pulled me close. His penis brushed the bone of my hip, then nestled in the hollow between my hip and stomach. He pressed himself against me, his hands and body working even in sleep, then he rolled on top of me, straining, his penis pushing at my skin. Humping. I clung to him, riding him even though I was underneath, pressing myself against him and imagining what it would be like if he were inside me. The pleasure of his skin on mine, the pressure, and the motion were intense. The fantasy that he was between my legs, that he was sliding in and out of me, was vivid.

"Connor," I said without thinking.

He jerked awake and scrambled to one side, shaking his head. "Lila? My god, I thought you were a dream." He put his hands to his face. "I'm so sorry."

He seemed to feel he had wronged me somehow, and I had no words to explain how wrong he was, or why I was there, since I couldn't really explain it to myself, either. So I played the part of the wronged woman and fled back to my bedroom. Eventually, I slept in spite of myself.

This time I woke with the windows in shadow, the afternoon light muted by the fog. By the time I showered and dressed, sunset was happening on the other side of the mist, and I came down to the kitchen to find Connor reading the newspaper and eating a piece of toast with marmalade just like it was breakfast time. He stood up when I came in, one of those Old World habits I didn't understand. Did it mean we were back on formal terms? Or as formal as we could be, since he was still wearing a bathrobe?

"The water's hot," he said, indicating the kettle.

I ignored it and went for the coffeemaker, filling the pot from the sink and pouring it into the open lid. When it began to perk, I sat down at the butcher-block table across from him.

"How are you feeling?" he asked, his hands quiet in his

lap now even though he had a piece of half-eaten toast on his plate and a half-empty cup of tea on the table. His attention was fully on me.

"All right," I said, resenting his solicitous tone, the distance in his voice.

"Look, if you want me to go, I understand. "

"Shut up," I said, relishing the American-ness of the phrase, the way it sounded coming out of my mouth. "Just be quiet for a minute while I try to say what I want to say. I get all mixed up with you and your expectations sometimes I don't even say or do what I really want." Not just his, I realized. Everyone's.

He just nodded at that, his lips pressed tight.

"I want you, Connor. I really, really want you. I don't have an explanation for it—call it chemistry or whatever—fine. I think it's obvious you want me, too. I think we both know how much it's going to hurt to just walk away from that." I already had an ache in my stomach, another one dead center in my chest, just thinking about the possibility that he might leave. "I know neither of us wants to hurt Jim, either, but . . ." I threw up my hands and let them land in my lap like his. "There's got to be a way we can do this."

And so he said it. "Just tell me the rules, Lila. Just tell me the rules." The rules. I couldn't articulate them last night and still couldn't now. But when he said that, I knew he meant it: I was in charge. I didn't like that feeling as much as I had liked the thrill and questions and wondering how far he would go the night before. I didn't like it as much as knowing I could blame him for anything that happened. But

I liked it better than thinking I might never get to touch that velvet silk cock of his again.

I stood up, and he did, too, and I went around the table to stand as close to him as I could get without touching him. "I'm not experienced like you," I said. "I don't know what to say is okay and what is not okay, other than the obvious."

"What is the obvious?" he said, so close my hair moved a little in his breath.

"Your penis doesn't go in my vagina." The coffeepot gurgled and sighed—it was ready. "Beyond that . . . we'll see."

He swayed just a centimeter, holding himself back. "It'll be up to you to tell me when to stop, then."

"Yes, I suppose it will."

"Are you sure you can do that?"

I wasn't, but I said, "Yes."

"May I kiss you now?"

I tipped my face upward. "If you ask me if every single thing is okay, I will kill you."

He gave a nod and then closed the distance between our lips. I gasped, realizing that for all we had done the night before, we had not kissed. His tongue moved urgently, coaxing mine to meet its desire, rough and delicious. And there he was again at my neck, making my knees give way. This time he carried me to his room and sat me on the edge of the bed as he pushed the covers aside. I got out of my own clothes and helped him fling the bathrobe away, and got a good look at him nude for the first time.

His erection was just beginning to rise, and I realized the extra softness of him I had felt was his foreskin. I had never touched a man who wasn't circumcised before. He watched me watching him harden and was about to say something when I reached out and gripped it gently, tugging him toward me, until I could lick him, soft and delicious. I worked my way up and down the length of him, until I could take him into my mouth, letting him plumb the softness of my cheek, then my throat, with restrained thrusts of his hips. I felt as if I were memorizing the shape of him, and again I imagined what it would be like to have him sliding inside me for real. I whimpered thinking about it.

He broke away from me then with a gasp, and I saw his cock spasm but not spurt before he pressed me back against the sheets, covering my body with his, pressing my hands down with his, licking my neck, then my breasts, nipping at my nipples with his teeth, and making me jump and writhe underneath him. He slid down then, and buried his face between my legs, that urgent tongue now searching through the folds of my labia, tweaking my clit until he settled into a gentle sucking and licking rhythm. I could feel his fingers playing around the edges of my hole, the dripping wetness, as he lapped and sucked, his tongue occasionally clucking.

"Put your finger inside," I said.

He looked up, his eyes just meeting mine over my heaving belly, questioning.

"Go ahead," I insisted. "I want your finger inside me."

He seemed to nod while continuing to work his mouth, and his fingers circled and teased as they had before. I curved my hips upward, trying to slide myself onto one of them, vainly. Then finally he did it, sliding a finger all the way in, making a circular motion as he did, and I cried out. My mouth remembered the shape of him, and I pretended it was his cock going in down there, plunging wet and bare inside me. He quickened his pace, both his mouth and his thrusts, and it was not long before my orgasm blossomed. Each thrust seemed to send waves of pleasure out from my center, making my nipples pucker and my hair stand on end. This time he did not let up on my clit until three, maybe four more orgasms had passed, and I pushed at his forehead with my hands to finally bring the round to a close.

And then he was kissing me, with that salty, sloppy mouth—I was licking at him and devouring him as the aftershocks pressed my body harder against him. I felt him shudder.

"You have to come this time," I told him. "I want you to."

"I want to, too," he said, rolling onto his back.

"Let me do it," I said, straddling him.

"As you wish, madam."

I took him in my hands, both hands, stroking him up and down. If I scooted forward a little, I could get the wet part of my crotch up against him . . . there. I pressed forward until my cunt lips were pressed against the base of him, my clit up against the ridge that ran along the underside of his penis. I slathered him wet, sopping the loose foreskin with my juices and enjoying the feeling of that hard pole in the middle of all that softness.

"Lila," he said, in an "are you sure" tone of voice.

"I know," I said, just to shut him up. I pulled one of his hands toward me, put his thumb against my clit. It was an impractical position—our wrists banging together as I stroked him against me, but we made a go of it anyway. After a few minutes of that, though, he said, "I can rub you without going inside you, if that's what you want."

I merely nodded and moved onto my back. He settled his cock between my cunt lips again, and I stifled a laugh thinking of a hot dog in a bun, the last inch of it sticking out. Then he began to grind and the laughter turned to a gasp. His arms shook but he held himself up, thrusting in a sudden fast spurt, then slowing down for long strokes, then again the sudden double-time, triple-time. I hadn't quite expected it, but I suddenly realized he could make me come this way, and I told him so.

"Then I want to come with you," he said, his dark curls stuck to his face with sweat. "If that's all right."

I may have gotten out a sound of assent, or maybe it was just me grunting as he redoubled his efforts, crushing me, bruising me on my own pelvic bone, a sensation I craved even though I had never known it before. My clitoris was smashed, twisted, under him, as he stroked himself on my flesh, no more slowing down now, only the hungry, desperate rhythm as he neared his climax. I began to come, my eyes clenched tight as I tried to will him to arrive as well, the sparks shooting through my nerves with every crushing thrust.

And then there was hot, wet semen spilling onto my stomach, and Connor exclaiming wordlessly. Then his arms gave out and he fell in a heap on top of me. We lay like that, breathing in and out, for a while, while I tried to think of something to say.

Eventually what I thought of, and said, was this. "Jim comes home in ten days."

"I know," he said. "Will you have had enough of me by then?"

"I don't know," I said.

"I'll do my best to make sure you have," he answered, and buried his face in my neck. "Just tell me when you're sick of me."

"Not yet," I told him, and pressed his head against me as he began to suck and lick me again.

THE NEW WORLD

Simon Sheppard

Jakov looked out the window. Hester Street was full of life that Friday afternoon: shopkeepers, businessmen, mamas doing their before-Sabbath shopping, vendors with pushcarts full of vegetables or dry goods, girls playing ringalevio, boys hawking the *Jewish Daily Forward* on the street corners, and a few identifiable ne'er-do-wells. The tumult of the Lower East Side: July heat rose from the streets, carrying the smells of cooking food, unwashed flesh, horse-shit, and flowers. And then he saw him, down in the street. Jakov could feel his crotch swelling . . . and his heart, as well. It was, indeed, the land of liberty. And it hadn't been so long since he'd arrived. Since *they'd* arrived, he and Simcha. Not long at all, really, though sometimes it seemed an eternity.

The ship had been on the ocean for over a week, with nearly a week still to go. It had been the worst two days out of England, when rough weather had hit. Below deck in steerage, where hundreds of immigrants were packed together, praying and crying and being sick, things went from bad to hellish, the stench of vomit mixing with the reek of unwashed bodies.

Jakov hadn't been able to sleep much since they'd left land, and though the ship bucked miserably upon the waves, he lay down in his bunk, his head on his tattered suitcase, and let sleep overtake him in the middle of the day. Sometime later— was it minutes or hours?—he awoke.

"Sleep well?" The boy who asked the question was lying in the bunk beside Jakov's, looking straight at him with soft, dark eyes. Something within Jakov stirred, some strange feeling.

Jakov answered back in Yiddish, the same as the boy's question. "As well as I could, under the circumstances."

The two talked for hours. Unlike Jakov, who was a farm boy, Simcha had come from a city, Kraków. He'd been studying for the rabbinate when his father, a merchant with a penchant for gambling, died, plunging his family into poverty. He was going to America to get a good job, provide for his mother and sisters, and, he hoped, eventually send for them so they could join him in New York.

Jakov was on his own, too. His parents, alarmed by a constant drumbeat of anti-Semitism, ground down by life on an impoverished farm, had scraped together what money they could and sent their only child to a land of promise and peace. "But now I don't know," Jakov said. "I miss them, I miss my home, and I'm all alone." He felt as if he might cry.

Simcha reached over and gently touched Jakov's shoulder. "Don't worry," he said. "You're not all alone anymore. Now you have me."

It was a fine sentiment, a noble sentiment. Elevated. So why, Jakov wondered, had his penis gotten hard at Simcha's touch?

Though the seas had grown calmer, Jakov's heart was stormy, filled with longing for Simcha. It was troubling. It was most likely a sin. And it was thrilling.

The next night, after the men around him were snoring heavily, Jakov, still awake, reached over to the next bunk. His fingers brushed against the rough wool of Simcha's blanket. Slowly, slowly, he moved his hand beneath the bed covers, so nervous he could barely breathe. He could feel the heat from the boy's body. As if swept along in a trance, he moved his hand till he touched Simcha. His hand was on Simcha's underwear, and that perfect moment was all he ever wanted. It was every moment in his life that had been filled with delight, combined. It was even more. Afraid to go further, unwilling to turn back, Jakov let his hand just sit there against the boy's side, feeling the warmth of his body, as the ship that bore them onward to who-knows-what was rocked by the endless ocean.

And that was when everything—the whole world—changed. Simcha grabbed Jakov's wrist, grabbed it hard. Found out, Jakov felt his face flush hot. But instead of pushing Jakov's hand away, Simcha drew it toward him, down his body, over his belly, down to the burning heat of his crotch. Jakov felt the alien hardness through the fabric and closed his hand around it. Only then did Simcha let go, darting his hand out from beneath the covers and stroking Jakov's curly black hair.

Hardly able to believe he was doing it, Jakov relaxed his hand, pulled at the buttons of the fly, and slid his fingers beneath the cloth. The flesh of the young man's penis was hot and moist, almost sticky, delectable, the pubic hair wiry against his hand. Jakov knew that even touching himself was supposed to be a sin, so this could only be a thousand times worse. A million. Still, feeling Simcha's hand on his face made it all seem somehow good. He ran his fingers up and down the swollen shaft and, alarmingly, Simcha moaned. Had anyone heard? No, no . . .

At that moment, the ship began to pitch. The man in the bunk above Jakov's coughed and tossed in his sleep, his arm flopping down over the edge, his hand nearly hitting Simcha's arm. Jakov jerked his hand back and hurriedly rolled over, turning away from Simcha.

Jakov lay on his sweat-soaked mattress, breathing heavily, his hand burning with the memory of Simcha's heat. How did it happen? How could it have happened? And what might it have led to if they hadn't had to stop? Despite his fears, his piercing sense of guilt, he wanted more. He wanted Simcha, all of him. It took him a long, long time to get to sleep that night.

———————————

Simcha and Jakov spent all the next day together. They talked about their families, their fellow passengers, their hopes for their lives in America, everything but what had happened the night before.

Jakov found it all—what he felt for Simcha, what he'd done with him the night before—very troubling. He knew that the rabbi he'd met onboard, who'd come from two towns over from his own, would never approve, that his fellow villagers would have beaten him if he'd been found out doing something like that back in Poland. But whenever he decided to tell Simcha that he never wanted to touch him again, even that they should switch bunks with other passengers, he'd look into his new friend's deep, dark eyes, and his resolve would vanish, escaping over the endless water all the way to the American horizon.

That evening Simcha proposed a walk on the deck. It was chilly outside, and near deserted, except for those avoiding the stale-food-and-sweat smells of steerage, and the people being noisily sick over the rail. Somewhere, faintly, a woman was singing a Yiddish lullaby.

"It's not wrong, you know," Simcha said, as if he could read Jakov's mind. Jakov said nothing, so Simcha continued. "There were places in Kraków where men . . . like us could go."

Jakov looked out at the stars, and a shiver went through his body, not necessarily from the cold. "It doesn't matter," he said weakly.

Simcha grabbed him by the elbow and drew him into the shadows, where nobody else could see. Simcha pressed his body against Jakov, who, despite feeling he *should* resist, was thrilled by the contact, his erection throbbing beneath his serge trousers.

"It's not wrong," Simcha repeated. He leaned over and kissed Jakov's cheek.

No one had ever kissed Jakov before, except his mother and a couple of aunts. But his aunts' attentions had been soft and bothersome. The firm touch of Simcha's lips was quite something else, something thrilling, disturbing, and new. Impulsively, Jakov reached up and stroked his friend's face. Simcha's lips found his, Simcha's tongue burrowed its way inside his mouth. It all felt so strange and terrifying, and Jakov wanted it never to stop. But then there were voices nearby, and Simcha gently pulled away. "Perhaps we should go," he said. "It's freezing out here."

As they walked back toward steerage, Jakov's hands thrust into his pants pockets to camouflage his still-erect shaft, they passed the people they'd heard, a young man and woman walking arm in arm. *Like us,* Jakov thought, *and yet not like us at all.* He felt like crying and laughing and praying, all at once. It was as if he were going crazy. The waves lapped endlessly against the ship that was carrying them to the New World.

———————————

That night, Jakov had a vivid dream. He and Simcha were on deck, not steerage deck, but the main deck, where the well-to-do passengers strolled. But no one else was there, just the two of them, even though the Statue of Liberty had come into view. The two stood hand in hand at the rail, the generous sun pouring down on them. They were joyful at their first sight of America, at the ending of their long and arduous passage.

"Let's go," Simcha said.

"What? Where?"

"Let's go. Freedom. Why wait?"

Simcha clambered over the rail and pulled them both overboard. Still hand in hand, they fell, plunging together toward the waves. But it wasn't a frightening feeling, it was a comforting one, and when they hit the water, it wasn't freezing. It was warm as a bath.

And now that they were in the ocean, they were naked. They plummeted downward, still holding hands, able to breathe underwater. Naked, Simcha was even more beautiful, his lithe body almost hairless except for a sprinkling of dark hair between his nipples, coarse black fur covering his legs, a big dark bush above his long cock. They released their hands and began to swim, swirling around one another in the comforting water, their journey at an end. Jakov floated on his back beneath the waves. Above him, the Statue of Liberty's image rippled down through the surface of the harbor, wavering, breaking apart, then joining together again. As Jakov lay beneath the waves, Simcha swam over and embraced him, his thin body gliding over Jakov's stockier peasant physique. Their erections sought each other, rubbing together, filling Jakov's body with a strange ecstasy. Fish became ribbons became bubbles became light. Jakov shook off Simcha's grip and, with a stroke of his arms, swam down to Simcha's crotch. Opening his mouth, he took Simcha's penis inside, the salty water mingling with the sweet taste of flesh. It was glorious for a few moments, but then the trouble began. He could hardly breathe, he was choking, drowning. He tried to push Simcha away, but the boy kept thrusting into his mouth, down his throat. Jakov was desperate now, thrashing about, struggling for breath. Whimpering, he began to black out.

When he opened his eyes, he was back in steerage, surrounded by the stench of stale bodies and the snores of sleeping men. It took a few moments for him to shake free of the dream, to realize that, to his mortification, he'd ejaculated onto his mattress. He looked over at Simcha, who slept soundly, looking innocent. Feeling miserable and confused, Jakov rolled over and went back to sleep in his wet, sticky bed.

For the masses packed together in steerage, the days were slogging by. Hopeful expectations of arrival were crushed beneath the numbing discomforts of the voyage. Tempers grew short. Fights broke out. One elderly man's heart gave out as he argued with his wife.

And within Jakov, too, a battle raged. Nothing had ever made him as happy as being with Simcha, nothing had ever gotten him as excited. Just accidentally brushing up against him or feeling Simcha's hand on his arm sent delicious thrills through his body . . . and gave him an erection. But there was his duty: to his family, to the Jewish community, to God.

"I'm sure if Elohim had not wanted us to feel this for each other," Simcha said once, "then He would not have made us this way." But that wasn't rationalization enough, not for what Jakov was feeling. More than once, he'd decided it was all a mistake, that the only thing to do was make a clean break. He would act coldly toward Simcha, sometimes snap at him and stalk away, and if he dared look back, he would see his friend standing there with sad, puzzled eyes. At such times, though torn, he'd remind himself that right was right, that he would have to be strong, to ignore the troubled yearnings of his heart and be a man.

But then there were those moments, times when he couldn't resist—furtive gropings after the lights went out, dangerous kisses in some shadowed corner—that made Jakov feel more than alive. Perhaps once the *Leeds Castle* reached land and he was free of this metal prison in the middle of the sea, the forbidden desires would vanish and he would be able to forge a new life in a strange land, untroubled by thoughts of Simcha's touch. But, increasingly, he was coming to doubt that. Sometimes he would go up on deck alone and stare out at the water, and wonder if he shouldn't throw himself overboard for real, putting an end to this agony. But suicide, too, would be a sin.

And then he would run into Simcha, and the morbid thoughts would vanish in a rush of desire, and all he would want was to see Simcha naked at last, to hold his body against his own, to kiss him until their swollen penises brimmed over and their bodies were bathed in each other's juices. What more was there to say, to think about, than that?

Late one morning, the long-awaited moment came: The Statue of Liberty had been sighted. Everyone rushed to the rail. Old men muttered prayers, women in babushkas wept, and Simcha and Jakov stood side by side, their knuckles covertly brushing each other's hands.

Once the ship was docked at Manhattan, the steerage passengers waited, huddled together, baggage in hand, till the upper-class passengers had disembarked. Then they got off the ship and onto a ferry to Ellis Island. When the ferry had docked, Simcha and Jakov clambered off, their feet on American soil at last. Surrounded by the mob from their ship, they made their way to the Main Building, then up the staircase to the cavernous Registry Hall. The guards shoved them, shouted commands at them, and pinned numbers to their chests. The immigrants were fed through a maze of iron-railed passageways. Overcome with fatigue from the voyage, Jakov felt faint. He looked over at Simcha, who said softly, "It will be all right, I swear to you, my love."

Love! It was the first time Simcha had uttered the word, and it made Jakov's heart both sink and fly, soar and drown.

"We'll find a little place together, Jakov, and . . ."

"No," Jakov said.

"What?" Simcha sounded baffled.

"I said no. It's over. What happened, happened, but now we're in America. It's time we acted like men." Jakov lingered behind, hoping Simcha would be carried along by the crowd, be swept out of his troubled life. But Simcha refused to move, so eventually Jakov grimly stumbled ahead, past feeble old men with parcels and young, hopeful families stinking of dirt. Somewhere in the clamor, he thought he heard Simcha crying out his name, but he had to stay resolved. He had to.

He shuffled through the passageways till he reached the medical examiners. He got prodded and poked, and then was shoved along. It was only then that he allowed himself to look back. Simcha was being examined, but something was different, something was wrong. The medical examiner chalked an unreadable word on his tattered jacket, and then two guards led Simcha away.

They might never see each other again. Never.

Suddenly frantic, Jakov managed to find a guard who spoke Polish. "My friend . . ." he stammered. "They took him away . . ."

"Is he related to you?"

How could Jakov possibly explain? "No, but . . ."

"Well, then, I'm sorry but there's nothing that can be done." The guard turned away and walked off.

Jakov could feel his heart breaking. He answered an inspector's questions, was issued a landing card, and was ferried to the mainland, water churning in the boat's wake. He was headed for the promised land, but he was, again, all alone.

Manhattan was far taller, grimier, and noisier than any place he'd ever been. But Jakov had a responsibility to his family, and to himself, to make a go of it. And to Simcha, too. He got a place in a rooming house—a private room, but little more than a closet, really, with a single small window overlooking the fire escape—and found a job hauling ice: tiresome, backbreaking work. He still dreamed of Simcha, whether he was asleep or awake, but it was already surprisingly hard to remember all the details of his face, a face he'd gazed on so many times and thought he knew so well. Now it shifted and broke apart in his memory, as though he were underwater, looking up past the surface at the man he . . . loved.

His desires were still there, despite the rigors of finding his place in the tumult of New York. When he went to the bath house to cleanse himself, he would find himself embarrassingly excited by the sight of other men undressing. He would have to flee, wrapped in a towel, to the precincts of the *shvitz,* where old men sat steaming themselves, gossiping loudly in German, Polish, Yiddish, Russian. Fearful of betraying himself, he cut back his visits to the baths and began to reek.

Sometimes he'd wander several blocks west, to the Italian neighborhoods, where, he'd heard rumors, men practiced "unnatural vices," and where, sure enough, he spotted handsome young fellows on street corners waiting, or so it seemed, to be hired for sex. One time a pair of chattering, effeminate Italian boys had flown out of a saloon on Elizabeth Street, almost running into him. They'd looked straight into his eyes with a blend of impudence and desire. Then one of the fairies said "Kike" and they flounced off down the block, leaving the smell of cologne in their wake.

And when he was troubled, or lonely, or sad, filled with regret or just unable to sleep, he'd lock the door of his little room, turn off the light, and, struggling to recall each detail of Simcha's face, masturbate in the dark. The pleasure, no matter how brief, was comforting, but it also made it too clear that Simcha wasn't there, was no doubt back in Poland by now. It was unlike him to think in such terms, but Jakov felt like part of his heart was missing. He would try to imagine the two of them together as he stroked himself, and sometimes, just before he came, he would murmur Simcha's name.

April turned to May, May to June. Life in America went onward. Jakov had even managed to send a little money back to his parents, who had sacrificed so much so he could get to America. And then, one hot, humid evening, Jakov had just gotten home from delivering ice, his undershirt soaked with sweat, when the landlady, Mrs. Ringelblum, delivered a message. "A young fellow came by for you earlier. He didn't give his name; he said you'd know who he was. And he said he'd come back later tonight. Remember, no guests in the rooms after ten o'clock."

"Thin? Dark, curly hair?" That description fit most all of the young men on the Lower East Side.

But Mrs. Ringelblum was already heading back down to her apartment, through hallways thick with the miasma of boiling cabbage.

It couldn't be Simcha . . . but it had to be.

Jakov would have gone to the baths to wash himself, but he was afraid he'd miss Simcha's second visit. So he waited around in a state of almost unbearable anticipation. Whatever guilt he'd felt, whatever doubt, was nothing in the face of his hunger to see Simcha again. He barely touched his dinner, then went upstairs to wait. Around eight o'clock, there was a knock on his door.

Hardly able to breathe, Jakov turned the doorknob. Simcha.

"But how . . . how . . ."

"It wasn't easy to find you, believe me," Simcha smiled. "But I did. As you can see."

"And what happened at Ellis Island? I thought for sure you'd been sent back to Poland."

"Something about my eyes, some infection, they thought. They kept me for a week, then let me enter the country."

Jakov felt tears welling up in his own eyes, running wetly down his cheeks. "Simcha . . ."

"I know. I know. Shhh. Don't cry. Don't cry."

Simcha locked the door behind himself, then walked to the window and drew the curtain.

That was the first night that Jakov saw Simcha naked, watched him strip down and stand before him, his penis rising stiffly, his chest mostly smooth and his legs hairy, like in the dreams. Jakov thought—no, knew—he'd never seen anything so beautiful.

Wordlessly, Simcha got down on the bed on all fours and offered up the dark, hairy crack of his ass. Jakov tore off his own clothes, buttons clattering to the floor, and knelt behind Simcha. He grabbed the boy's buttocks and spread them, spitting on the hole. But then, with the head of his cock ready to enter Simcha, he hesitated, wondering if it was somehow wrong—that this was one voyage he ought not embark on after all—until Simcha softly begged him to go on, to please go ahead. With a grunt, Jakov maneuvered his hard, thick flesh into the boy's wet heat, and they both gasped. He looked down. He was inside Simcha, actually inside him.

"Am I doing it right?" Jakov asked.

Simcha could barely get the words out: "Fine, just fine."

As Jakov thrust in and out, he reached down around Simcha's waist: The beautiful boy's beautiful penis was still rock hard, dripping. He plunged into Simcha with sudden ferocity, yearning to escape into some explosion of joy and lust, even if it meant damnation itself.

"Ow," said Simcha. "Ow ow ow." But it was too late:

They'd come too far. Too far. Jakov couldn't hold back. He wouldn't hold back, not anymore. He would—he thought a word he shouldn't—fuck the boy, fuck him like he was a girl, better, like he was life itself.

"Please, please . . ." Simcha begged.

Too far. Jakov slammed into Simcha even harder. It all felt so amazing that he couldn't help himself. Moaning, he shot off deep into his lover, into the darkness, into the heat. Then he pulled his shaft out, shoved Simcha onto his back, leaned down, and sucked Simcha's hardness into his mouth. Within moments, the boy's juices swept over his tongue: surprising tasting, a little bitter, a little like the ocean, but he swallowed it thirstily down.

"Damn," said Simcha, when they'd both finally caught their breath, and he was lying in the crook of Jakov's arm, his head nestled on the young man's muscular chest, "you smell awful. Worse than you did on the ship." He turned, put his face in Jakov's furry armpit, and inhaled deeply. And they both laughed.

And then, when the laughter was over, Jakov felt suddenly, deeply guilty, as though the whole world were a dark, empty place, until Simcha reached up and stroked his face, and everything was once again peaceful and fine.

Simcha already had a place around the corner, sharing with two other young men. Jakov's room would have been too small for both of them, anyway. But night after night, whenever he could, Simcha came to Jakov's little room and the two of them made love. Simcha was there so often that dumpy Mrs. Ringelblum even began to refer to him as "your best friend." Did she know, or at least suspect? It was less than unlikely.

Simcha was reluctant to tell Jakov what he did for money, and Jakov, who knew that some of the new arrivals were involved in criminal gangs, didn't press the point. But Simcha sometimes had enough extra money so that he could take Jakov out to eat at the dairy restaurant on the corner of Orchard and Delancey, or, dressed up in their best clothes, to a show at the Yiddish theater. To the world, they must have looked like a couple of young bachelors out for a pleasant night on the town, waiting for the right women to come into their lives. Only they knew different.

The tumult of the Lower East Side: Summer heat rose from the streets, carrying the smells of cooking food, unwashed flesh, horseshit, and flowers. And when he saw Simcha down in the street, coming in his direction, Jakov could feel his penis swelling. Because it was a national holiday and the next day was *shabbos,* as well, Jakov had gotten half the day off.

Originally they'd talked about going down to the waterfront but then thought better of it: The streetcars would be jammed. Instead, Simcha knelt down and licked and sucked Jakov, meanwhile stroking himself until they both came, and then they got dressed and went up on the roof.

The sun was setting over Manhattan, over its towers and slums and the hordes of people all rushing madly on their way. And when it was dark, the two young men stared in the direction of the Statue of Liberty as fireworks filled the sky. They might be in a land where many people hated them for what they were—for *all* of what they were. Their families would be heartbroken, the rabbis would disapprove. But for the glorious moment, none of that mattered, none of it. Jakov smiled at Simcha, Simcha smiled back, and they held hands in the dark, high above Hester Street.

ENTRY POINT

Shanna Germain

I've never done this before: the warm wooden paddle gripped in my fists, the canoe that shivers and thrusts beneath me every time I shift in the seat, my husband behind me, guiding us. From the canoe ahead of us, our daughter turns, lifts one hand off her paddle and waves. She is watching out for us; it was her idea to bring us here, hers and her friend's, to the middle of the Adirondacks, where we will paddle and camp our way down this miles-wide river.

Susan lifts her head beneath her ball cap. The cap, brown with blue lettering, reads "Kiss My Bush." A few years ago, I would have asked her to take it off. For her father's sake more than mine. He's no supporter of Bush, of course, but he's no supporter of "sportin' your business everywhere" either. It makes me laugh, the pun of it all, but I can't imagine wearing something like that. I didn't even get one of those "Women

Against the War" pins, although I'd wanted one. I knew I would have just put it in my drawer, and what was the sense of that?

Now, I just smile and take my own wet, cool hand off the paddle and wave back. If he wants Susan to take the hat off, he'll have to tell her himself. Susan smiles—it still knocks my heart back when she smiles, three dimples—cheek, cheek, and chin—like a perfect right triangle, like a constellation in a day sky.

Susan gives me a thumbs up, a "you're being a real trooper, Mom," sign and then turns back around. Her friend, no, her partner—partner, I still have to get used to saying that word, to thinking that thought—paddles with long, efficient strokes. Reese. She is tall and thin and pale, the muscles in her bare shoulders moving like miniature pistons with each sweep of the paddle.

They are efficient together—paddling on one side and then the other, switching at some rhythm known only to them, Susan sometimes holding the paddle in the water against the boat, bringing the front of the canoe to one side or the other. They could outrun us, with our halting strokes and fat canoe, with the way Harry steers by waiting until we're close enough to the bank to push off on something. But they don't, they stay nearby as though it is only their inability to go faster and not their fear for the old folks that keep them here. It makes me grateful in my heart for them, for both of them, for Susan, for Reese being the one she chose.

"What you doing, Lese?" Harry's voice at my back, his paddle, swish swish into water. "You plan on making me do all the work back here?"

I take the paddle off of my knees, dip it into the water. "I was thinking about it," I say. I like the way my voice sounds, the smooth sharp youth that has come into it since we got here. My comeback sounds like the crunch and snap of a green twig.

Harry nudges my back with the end of his paddle. I can barely feel it through the thick life vest. "Watch it up there," he says. "I've got a mind to make you steer."

We both know that he would do no such thing. He is a gentleman, Harry, through and through. He holds doors and buys flowers and doesn't say "damn" in mixed company. This is what I fell in love with forty years ago. The first time I went out with him, we were walking to the movies and the rain started falling down around us. He didn't wait one second before he was out of his coat and laying it across my shoulders to keep my dress dry. It wasn't the coat I remember so much as the way he put his arm there too, keeping the coat on my shoulders, giving me the warmth of his skin, never once trying to touch me wrong. He left his coat, and his arm, there all day, all through the movie and the way home. When he left me on the porch, saying good night, and taking back the things that were rightfully his—his coat, his arm—it was the first time I'd felt naked in my whole life.

'Course the something that makes you fall in love with someone can be the same thing you come to hate. This gentleman thing of Harry's, the way he would never say a bad word to anyone. The way he wouldn't get his dander up, not even when he should have. Like when Susan was a teenager, running wild and rampant in the streets, and all he could do was offer her a cup of tea and a towel when she came home. But I'm used to it all over again now, I guess. Now that we're old, I like that arm around my shoulder, the way he does it without thinking.

When the only sounds are water and birds and the slow steady stream of air going past, there's not much else to do but paddle and breathe. Up ahead, Susan and Reese move in their special rhythm. Geese create a V overhead; fall is coming. I don't know how they know—you can't feel it in the air yet. Down here on the river, it's still summer, with the lilies and the water skimmers and the trout who raise their big mouths up to the sky. I can't believe in all our forty years, Harry and I have never done this. Sure, we've done lots of things, broader, wider things. Moved to the West Coast once for about six months, while Harry worked and Susan toddled around the new house, pulling herself from box to box. And we took that trip to France a few years back, cute hotels and food so rich you could just feel it giving your heart a workout. But we've never done this, such an easy thing: drive on up to the most beautiful area in the state, rent a canoe, fit your palm around a wooden oar. Never thought to do it, I guess.

Susan and Reese slow down until they're alongside us. "Put your paddles up," Susan says. Then she reaches out to grab the side of the canoe with wet fingers. A diamond flashes on her middle finger, a gift from Reese. Susan called it a commitment ring. Like a cross between engagement and marriage.

We float that way a while, listening. Dark is falling somewhere nearby. You can see it in the way the shadows lengthen on the river, the way the trees darken and reach.

Susan takes her hand off the boat, points to shore. "We're going to try and camp over there," she says. "Should be an easy landing."

It's not easy, but it's okay. Reese jumps into the river at mid-thigh, a little splash and sigh, and then she grabs the front of our canoe and pulls us ashore. Harry doesn't like that, being pulled to the sandy banks while he's sitting in the back with his oar on his lap, but he doesn't say anything. And by the time I've got the salmon and corn steaming over the campfire, he's helping the girls raise the tents. One on this side of the clearing, one on the other.

We eat around the campfire, gobbling in the near dark. I'm so hungry I eat the salmon with my fingers, pulling the greasy pink flesh off the bone and sticking it in my mouth.

Susan does the same. "Jesus, Ma, this it the best thing I've ever tasted."

"I agree," Reese says, her mouth so full of fish the words barely come out. I feel a quick surge of warmth toward her.

After dinner, Harry goes off into the woods to do his business somewhere quiet, and I sit on the picnic table, away from the campfire. The dark makes soft edges out of my fingers. Harry's footsteps are light across pine needles. He gives my shoulders a quick squeeze. "I'm gonna hit the hay," he says. His kiss is mint and river water and, somewhere beneath that, a hint of salty, sweet fish.

"'Night." I sit, watching the trees darken against the sky until I hear the zipper of the tent, the rustle of sleeping bag as Harry settles himself in like a dog. We didn't bring air mattresses or even good pillows—the canoe space was reserved for food and water and tents—and I imagine tomorrow we'll both be bent over and stiff from work and wear.

Across the campground, Susan and Reese are still sitting by the campfire, their backs to the picnic table. Together, near the flame, they are dark and light. Together, they should blot each other out. But they don't. Instead they make each other darker and lighter, luminescent, alive.

I watch as Susan leans into Reese, holding out a piece of fish between her fingers. Reese opens her mouth, takes the fish and Susan's fingers inside, holds everything there, her eyes on Susan's. Susan pulls her fingers out slowly, then she puts her fingers into her own mouth, sucks them the way she used to when she was a child. She'd get so excited by something—the tiger at the zoo, riding in the car, daddy coming home—that she'd stick her fingers in her mouth and suck on them, just to calm herself.

I don't believe they are being exhibitionists. They are just in their own world, not even aware that I'm watching.

Reese puts her palm against Susan's cheek, runs it up into Susan's ponytail. She pulls my daughter's face to her own. It is not gentle, and for one moment, I want to stand up, I want to slap this woman's face, tear her hand from my child's cheek. But then Susan closes her eyes, leans sideways into Reese's palm. Between their lips, the orange fire sparks and crackles.

When Susan opens her mouth against Reese's chin, I know I should turn away, but I cannot. There is something here that I am coming to understand. Something that is burning its way through my stomach, something that I am afraid of, something that I want. I am afraid that if I step back into the darkness now, that if I close my eyes without seeing my daughter's joy, if I unzip the tent and slide in beside Harry, that this everything will disappear. I want to capture this thing like a firefly, to bring it to Harry and say, here, look. To say, please, yes. But I am afraid that it will die between my cupped palms, that I will arrive at Harry's side with nothing more than a husk of something that was bright and shining.

Reese puts her palm against Susan's breast. Susan lets go of Reese's chin, lets her head fall back. In the darkness above the firelight, the exhale of her breath is clear and white. Reese leans forward, one thumb against Susan's breast, one hand against Susan's back, steadying her.

The thread of warmth inside me climbs up through my thighs into the bottom of my belly. When Reese ducks her head into the hollow space beneath Susan's chin, I force myself to get off the picnic table slowly, quiet. I will go to the tent. I will lie down beside Harry and put my arm across his belly and force myself to sleep. In the morning, I will get up and boil water for coffee and oatmeal over the campfire. Tomorrow, I will paddle with all my heart.

Still, Susan hears me. Her eyes, suddenly open, focus on my face. Reese, too, watching me, watching Susan, waiting to see what we will do. My cheeks flood with heat. I am an old woman in sweats, watching my daughter make love to another woman, living off her desires instead of my own.

Susan stares at me a moment longer. And then she smiles. Dimple, dimple, dimple. A constellation against the night sky. Stars to guide the way. "Sweet dreams, Ma," Susan says, and there is no shame in her voice, no humiliation. There is only my daughter, doing something she loves, wanting to share with me something that she loves. Pushing me, as she always has, to be something better, larger than myself. For her, this thing is no different than taking me canoeing. She is teaching me, watching out for me, taking me only as far as I can go. Then, she will let loose her hand, she will let me float. It is my job to do the rest.

"You too," I whisper. But she is already back in her own space, her mouth at Reese's ear, her hand on Reese's leg.

I make my way back to the tent by feel. The zipper sounds loud in the darkness. When I slide myself in, Harry is awake, waiting. "You okay?" he asks.

I nod, even though I know he can't see it. I slide into the double sleeping bag beside him and try not to shiver. He lays his arm across me, the same way he laid his arm across me when we were twenty. He doesn't even realize he's doing it, I don't think.

I start to say, "Harry, let's try something new." I start to say, "Harry, there's something I'd like to talk about." But I imagine his response, his patient listening, his arm across my shoulder, his gentlemanly ways, and I can't stand it.

Instead, I take his chin in my fingers and turn his head toward me. I am not gentle or kind. I am ravenous. I open my mouth over Harry's chin the way I'd seen Susan do with Reese. Harry's whiskers scrape my tongue, the sides of my gums. I taste his stubble, the spot in the middle of his bottom lip that always peels. My tongue is a fish inside him, entering new dark caverns, swimming to depths that I had forgotten existed. He tastes like Harry, but like something else, too—sweat and sea and salmon. I wonder what he tastes in me, what new flavors I might reveal.

There are too many layers between us—my sweats and his, the soft underskin of the sleeping bag. I slip my hands beneath his shirt, run them up the soft fur and flesh of his chest. My palm hits his nipple and Harry grunts, something like a porpoise, something like a wild animal.

"Shh," I say, but my shushing is louder than his noise. I run my thumb over his nipple again, the hardening point of it. Forty years, and I'm not sure if I've ever really felt his nipple before, the way its edges pucker like a berry, the way its peak rises beneath my skin. I circle my thumb again, and Harry moans inside my mouth.

I slide my hand out from his shirt, grip the waistband of his sweats. "Take these off," I say. I've never said this before, told him to undress, and the words taste strange in my mouth. I am not sure how he will react, but he does what I say, and fast, lifting his hips off the ground to get the sweats down. Then he sits up and pulls his T-shirt over his head.

"You too," Harry says, but his hands are already at my waistband, pulling my sweats down over my thighs. He only gets them down as far as my knees.

"Leave them," I say. I kick my legs until the sweatpants are in a pile at the bottom of the sleeping bag. I bring his head back toward me, enter his mouth with my tongue. Harry moans again, breath and noise against my tongue, the press and release of tides inside my body. I didn't know how much I loved the sound of him. I didn't know this sound *was* him—do I hear him now because we're in the quiet of the wilderness, or because I am listening hard here in the woods? I want to hear the sound again, feel that tide inside my body, so I run my thumb over his nipples, hard and fast, first one, then the other.

Harry pulls his mouth away from mine. Then he reaches for me, his fingers around my shoulder with some kind of force. He moves fast, faster than I remember, faster than I would have believed possible, and then he is above me, kissing me. Hard. He is not gentle. There is nothing gentlemanly about the way his tongue is in my mouth, hot and hard, the way his tongue runs across my teeth, the way his cock is pressing, insistent and wet as a dog's nose, against my thigh.

I wrap my hands around his cock, the long, sturdy, warm, living length of it. I roll it between my palms until his cock tightens and lengthens beneath my skin. Until Harry sighs, quiet as the woods, above me. If I had more courage, I would use all my strength to roll him over on his back, to press his shoulders down on the canvas floor of the tent and, beneath that, the rocks and sticks of the forest. I would raise myself above him, cup his cock in my hands. I would put my knees on either side of him and ride him. I would whisper *damn cock fuck* over and over in his ear.

But I am too old, too tired for that much courage. The light between my hands, between my thighs, is already waning. Instead, I take hold of his ass, the cool and wrinkled skin. I guide him between my thighs. Normally, I would let Harry take his time, let him take the time that he thought I wanted, needed. But not tonight, not here in the dark with my daughter out there. I am wet already with what I have seen, what I have grasped. The inside of my belly trembles like it's filled with fish and stream. I pull Harry into me, fast, sharp. He slides inside me so quickly that he gasps and falters. He opens his mouth. I am afraid he will apologize. He will ask if he's hurt me, and then all of this—this light, this heat, the hunger—will fall away.

Instead, he opens his mouth again to mine. He thrusts his tongue into me even as he thrusts his cock between my legs. And even as he does this, even as his cock enters me again and again, hard and hard, harder than I had hoped, than I had dreamed, even as the heat rises through my insides, I am grateful for this thing, this small precious gift that I have been given. For this heat, for this heated living thing between my legs.

"Yes," he says, and I'm not sure what he's saying yes to, if he even knows he's saying it, but I say yes too and then I am whispering it over and over, yes and yes and yes each time his cock sinks inside me. Even now his arm is over my shoulder, holding his body above me. I lean forward and open my mouth over the meat of his shoulder, let my teeth sink in a little. My mouth against his flesh still says yes and yes and yes, even as something drops through my middle, sending shivers out in all directions, leaving nothing but liquid and shine.

In the morning, I slip out of the tent while Harry sleeps, quiet, on his side. There is only our canoe waiting at the water's edge and a note scrawled in Susan's handwriting tucked beneath my oar. "Enjoy breakfast. Then get your butts in gear and catch up with us." I think of Susan and Reese, ahead of us, leading the way, believing in our ability to follow, to learn, to grow. I pick my oar up, think of the day opening ahead of us, the water and the woods. The oar reminds me of Harry's cock, the warmth and roll of it, the way it fits perfectly between my palms. I think today I will sit in the back. I think today I will learn how to steer.

FORGET-ME-NOT

Cheyenne Blue

Sarah and Liam spend a stolen summer week together in County Clare. They're walking the cliff tops and coastline, lacing their boots tight every morning and striding off into the mist, packs jiggling on their backs. It's Liam's idea, this secret week, and a perfect way of spending time together, one that will never be discovered.

Sarah's husband, Timothy, departed on a business trip to Hong Kong last Friday. He pecked Sarah on the cheek and told her to run along and enjoy the walking holiday with her girlfriend. "I've never been to Ireland," he said, although she knows that very well. He repeats small, trivial facts about himself on a regular basis, something she used to find endearing but now finds merely irritating.

Liam's wife, Aoife, thinks he's fishing on the Shannon with a German tourist he met last year. Aoife said she'd rather stay in Dublin, maybe visit her mother for a couple of days. Liam wonders if Aoife is having an affair as well—she agreed so swiftly to his going—but he doesn't really care enough to find out. They drift through the Dublin house on separate planes of existence, connecting briefly over the corn-flakes each morning before diverging again like blown leaves.

Liam and Sarah met two years ago, when her car broke down on an empty lane in County Tipperary. She was on a business trip from London, selling linen cloths and mono-grammed napkins to the country hotels. In time-honored fashion, Liam, who'd stopped to assist, invited her for a pint when he dropped her off at her hotel. That night, after the drinking and the flirting finished, he escorted her back to her room, followed her in, and pressed her up against the door, fucking her so hard that her back banged the door with every thrust.

Afterward, he touched her cheek with gentle fingers. "What have I done?" he murmured, his expression open and bewildered. "God help me, but I think I love you."

Tension shimmered between them, strung fine as a gos-samer thread, as real as the semen running down her thighs.

Sarah covered his hand with her own. "I don't know what we've started," she said. "But I feel it too."

She drew her business trip out for six more days. He told his wife about the chance of some carpentry work in the coun-try, and they spent six glorious days in Galway. Love, sudden sprung, unfurled in the rain and mist of the west. Hand in hand, they walked the streets of Galway town, drinking the black pints in small pubs, kissing with gentleness under the benevolent gaze of men in tweed caps. They would find a bed and breakfast, and love long into the night, uncaring of the squeaking springs, before rising too late for breakfast.

Since that first incandescent merging, there have been a few stolen weekends over the last two years, usually in Ireland; occasional nights in Edinburgh, when Sarah's business took her there, and Liam managed to get away and visit. Not much to keep a love affair alive.

But this time, they have a week. A whole week, one that is theirs alone, planned in advance, schemed and set up with the precision of a military campaign.

This holiday is for walking and for lovemaking. Every morning, Liam prods Sarah awake with his erection, rolling her over so that it bumps against her thighs. He kisses her mouth with sleep-slack lips, before moving down, nuzzling the curve of her neck and shoulder, down to where her ample white breasts spill softly on her chest. Her nipple blooms into his mouth, and he suckles lazily until, driven by his cock, he's compelled to advance.

Sarah tangles her hands in his hair, urging him to explore her breasts, meander down her belly, over the undulations, over the soft swell of it, to the thatch beneath. She spreads for him and directs his tongue with soft murmurs of appreciation.

When she has come good and fierce, convulsing under his fingers and tongue, he rises up and plunges into her. One stroke all the way in, battering her soft inner tissues in his enthusiasm. It never takes long, not in the mornings, and he comes with a moan, spilling himself inside her as she clenches around him.

They are always late for breakfast so must endure with grace the disapproving stares of the landladies. Sarah knows these frowning women sense they're not married to each other; she feels it in the way their gazes linger on her untamed hair and kiss-swollen lips.

Sarah and Liam love to walk, and by day they stride with rolling gait over the undulating cliff paths of Clare. The scenery is wild, windswept, and wet, and the rain often lashes them mercilessly, soaking through their waterproofs and plastering their jeans to their legs. But they don't mind; indeed, there are fewer people out in foul weather. The fair-weather tourists huddle in cafés with cups of tea, leaving the cliff tops for the brave.

He makes love to her on the edge of the world, where the land merges into the sea, the sheets of rain blurring the boundary. He peels off his clothes to feel the soft rain wash over his skin. The grass is springy here, yielding—like Sarah's thighs.

She's the aggressor this time, pushing him over onto his back and straddling him, sinking down onto his cock. Impatiently, she rips off her rain jacket and t-shirt, so that she's naked in the warm summer rain. It streams in runnels down her breasts, dripping off her nipples onto his chest. It's like tears, he thinks, the agony and the ecstasy of grief and love.

Sarah is as wet without as within. Liam runs his hands over her slick, wet skin. She's a selkie, a mer-child, head thrown back as she pants, grinding herself on his cock. Her hands rest on her thighs, and she raises and lowers herself in tidal rhythm. His cock surges, encased within her clasping heat, and he comes in a heated rush, and the wetness is absorbed into her body.

Afterward, they lie together, the sodden grass brushing damply over their skin. The seeds and green blades cling to them, so that they are patterned with nature. Below them, the sea surges against the rocks and a gull circles overhead, lazily arcing through the sky.

"Look," says Sarah. "Enough blue to patch a sailor's shirt."

She's right; there's a rent in the heavy sky, and they watch the blue expand until they are bathed in weak and watery sunshine. Sarah lies back, arms above her head, eyes closed. Her dark hair, entwined with clover and blades of grass, tangles around her neck.

He loves her like this, loves her more than his tidy wife in Dublin. Sitting up, he picks white clover, dandelions, and small blue flowers and threads them through her pubic hair, so that her thatch is a bed of wildflowers.

Rising up on her elbows, she studies his handiwork. "Forget-me-nots?" she asks, touching a blue flower with a fingertip.

"I won't," he swears, although it wasn't the question.

The sun sweeps away the clouds, and they sit naked on the cliff tops, watching the Atlantic heave beneath them.

"We should run away to America together," he says, as he stares out to sea.

"We should," she agrees, leaning against his shoulder, sifting the blonde hairs on his chest with her fingers.

He turns to her. "Tonight?" he asks. "We could live in New York. You could sell Irish linens to the fancy hotels there, and I could paint the Brooklyn Bridge over and over."

"We could," she says, kissing him with damp lips.

Liam knows it's make-believe to her, and the urge to convince her rises up strongly in his chest. He wants to prove his words with his body, with his possession of her, but she's scrambling up.

"People coming." She's fighting her way back into her knickers, pulling them up, bunching them so that his seed won't stain through to her jeans.

He dresses more leisurely, and by the time the middle-aged couple approaches, they're dressed, pulling on their day-packs.

Taking Sarah's hand, Liam curves her to his body. "Morning," he says to the couple, who nod and smile.

That day they walk eleven miles along the cliff tops, a long loop around the peninsula. When the rain threatens again, they stick their thumbs out on the road, and a farmer takes them into the nearest village. There's a pub, and a bed and breakfast that is full, but the landlady squeezes them into a small attic room under the roof, alive with the rustling sound of swallows nesting under the eaves.

After pints of porter and toasted sandwiches for supper, they retire to the narrow bed and fall into each other once more. Sarah buries her face in his belly, nuzzling the hairs, working lower to his twitching cock. She's in no hurry, taking her time, working careful fingers up his inner thighs, lightly brushing the hair on his balls before retreating.

He undulates his hips, angling them to entice her to taste. "Please," he begs. "Please."

The tip of her tongue laps him once, pushing into the slit of his cock, drawing up the fluid. The salt of his skin tastes like the salt of the sea, absorbed from the moisture-laden breeze. She doesn't like him to beg, so she takes him into her mouth without further ado, drawing him in, sweet suction and warmth. Sarah likes to do this for Liam; he tastes fresher, cleaner than her husband, and his skin is softer, as if the moist Irish air has filtered into him. She doesn't stop until he comes in her mouth, and his hoarse mumbles of gratitude bring a rush of tenderness.

Did he mean it about America, she wonders, as she wipes her mouth and presses him back against the pillow? Could they do this together? Is the love strong enough?

The rain is too heavy the next day, even for them, so they spend the day in bed and in the pub. The landlady smiles and offers them books and Scrabble. They play for a while—double points if the word is about love or sex—then brave the lashing rain to visit the pub. A turf fire burns merrily in the corner and they drink the porter once more, leaving slow, deliberate rings around their glasses like the locals do.

They talk to the middle-aged couple who nearly caught them in flagrante on the cliff the day before.

"How long have you been married?" the woman asks. "It's nice to see a couple still so much in love."

Sarah glances sidelong at Liam, then replies, "Fourteen years. We married when I was only nineteen."

He wonders if she really is thirty-three; they've never talked much about the mundane.

"No, no children," Sarah is saying, "but it's not for want of trying."

She runs a hand along his inner thigh, and with a jolt he realizes they won't stay in the pub for much longer. They'll brave the rain, retire to the room with the swallows, and make love once more. But the fantasy Sarah is weaving is a compelling one. She's telling her new friend about their home in County Offaly, where she works in the tourist information center, and how much she misses her dog, a terrier called Skipper. Lies, all lies.

He nearly drags her back to their room; he wants to be inside her again; it's where he belongs. She laughs at his desperation, smiling into his kisses and letting him pull her clothing aside, dragging her wet jeans down her legs. He pushes into her without foreplay, but it doesn't matter, she's soaked with arousal already, and he plunges once, one fierce thrust, biting her exposed breasts, leaving his mark on her skin.

"Careful," she warns. "I'll be home in three days. Timothy will be back."

"I don't care."

To her ears, his brogue has never been so pronounced.

"You're my woman. Mine." He bites again, and leaves a purple bloom on her white skin.

Anger rises in her suddenly, and she pushes at him. "Fuck off, Liam! This wasn't part of it."

He thrusts harder into her, pummeling her with fierce possession. "Nothing was said, no rules, no parameters. If I want to change them now, what's to stop me?" Gripping her hips, he pounds her with jackhammer strokes.

Sarah squirms. "Stop it! You're hurting me."

He slows, gentles, he doesn't want this to be about ownership. It's about love, and what it's doing to him. He kisses her mouth, which is pursed in anger. "I love you, Sarah. And I don't want you going back to him."

She is silent for so long that he thinks he's already lost the chance to claim her and spirit her away. They've said the words of love before, but never has the idea that there could be more than this entered into it.

"What about Aoife?" She won't meet his eyes, she's staring out of the window, watching the swallows dart under the eaves.

"She's a good wife," he says and winces. Such a condescending tone to his words, as if that is all Aoife will ever be in her life.

When she doesn't answer, Liam asks, "What about Timothy?"

Sarah's eyes are far away. Soft, misty looking. "Timothy is . . ." She pauses. "Timothy is a good husband."

And in the echo of his words he knows that this week is all there will be.

His erection withers, dies. Sarah shifts her legs, as if her hip is paining her, and he rolls off. It wasn't meant to be like this, he thinks. It was supposed to be something secret, something wonderful, something that he could hold to his heart when Aoife would barely raise her head from *The Irish Times* to acknowledge him.

But there's still three days left, and he still loves her. Deliberately, carefully, he smiles at her, bends his head to kiss her nipple, no purple marks this time. "Now," he says, "where were we?" His fingers skate over her belly to tangle in the soft, damp curls.

Sarah's eyes are distant, but as he parts her sex, fingers her with care, pushing one up inside her to curl around in the moisture and intimately stroke her, she returns to him.

Her sigh hovers in the room, and they draw back from the precipice they'd found themselves on, carefully, one step at a time.

His tongue replaces his fingers and he laps her, exploring the mossy cleft. He can smell sex in the hairs, musty from earlier, but he persists until fresh moisture rushes in, coating his tongue.

She comes with a long sigh, then turns to him, feeling for his dick, stroking him back to full hardness. This time, he's gentle with her, sliding inside, angling his strokes so that she moans with pleasure and pulls him further in by the buttocks.

Cupping the side of his face with her hand, she whispers, "I do love you, Liam, it's just that . . ." She cannot continue, as her orgasm washes over her, a dark crimson wave, and she drowns in its pleasure.

His own climax follows swiftly. They sleep close that night, caught up together, the sheets thrown back so that the moist eddies from the window caress their skin.

The next day they hold hands over breakfast, before shouldering their packs and striding off into the sunny morning.

This is all there is, thinks Sarah. It could never have been more than this. She watches the sea heave and thinks of the currents that will touch foreign shores.

Liam thinks of a fishing friend, a wise man, who once said to him, "Live your life to the cast, Liam. Bend your life to the whim of the wind." He tugs Sarah's hand more firmly into place and wraps his fingers tightly around hers, binding her to him for as long as the wind allows.

THE YACHT PEOPLE

Michael Hemmingson

1.

She didn't tell me she was a squirter. It's not the sort of thing an apparent one-night stand lets loose after a few drinks, some making out, the pulling off of the clothes, and the inevitable, eventual screw. I guess I can say it was a pleasant surprise, like the way a plumber grins when a pipe he's working on suddenly bursts.

There we were in my sailboat (a thirty-foot Catalina), squeezed onto my cabin bed; we were both half-naked, her legs were spread, and I was going down on her. I was having a fairly fun time eating her out, and then she shook and grunted and filled my mouth with her thick and tangy ejaculate.

There was a lot.

I mean *a lot.*

"Wow," I said, pulling back and spitting some of that wild stuff out.

"Sorry," she said rather seriously, grabbing at my hair like it was horse reins; "sometimes I get carried away when I get so excited."

Again I said, "Wow," with the wonder of a bright-eyed teenage football hero after his first blow job from a randy and dandy cheerleader.

Hey, it's the way I think, okay?

She asked, "Do you mind?"

"No; I like it."

"I bet you do," she said, "you *slut.*"

"What?"

"You heard me."

"Lady, did you just call me a 'slut'?"

"I *know* what you are," she said, "and my name is Erin. I'm hardly a lady, not in this position."

Erin, yes, Erin—I think she may have even told me that when I met her in the Yacht Club, adjacent to the Marriott Marina Hotel in downtown San Diego; you didn't have to live on one of the hundreds of boats docked at the marina to wine and dine and dance and mingle in the Yacht Club, although many of the people there at any given time of the day did own and live on a boat. I saw her there at the bar, or maybe she's the one who saw me; we'd crossed paths before. She sat down next to me, asked my name, and asked if I'd buy her a drink. "If you tell me yours," I said, being as coy as I could at the moment.

She misheard me. "If I show you mine? I need to have at least three strong drinks in my sexy flat stomach before I *show* it to you, buddy."

Actually, it was more like six, but who counts these days?

So there we were on my little boat—she showed me hers, I did my thing, she turned on the waterworks . . . and then I showed her mine.

"I always wanted to suck on a private dick," Erin said, reaching down and taking me in her mouth.

"Play with my balls, bitch," I told her.

She did with her long shiny fingernails.

2.

"Are you really a gumshoe?" she asked after I came in her mouth.

I was feeling pretty relaxed at the moment. I said, "Where did you hear that?"

"Gossip around the docks."

"Oh yeah?"

"People talk."

"They always do, don't they?" I had to smile. "The fuckers; the talking fuckers."

"I'm sure you've heard plenty of bad things about me."

"Not at all," I said, zipping my trousers up, "but I've just found out for *myself* just how juicy *you* can be."

She gave me this look, it was like *ha-ha*: I guess she didn't find my comment on her pussy flow amusing.

"No need to pout," I said.

"No need to be so *crude,*" she said. "So is it true? You're a private detective?"

"Was."

"You were fired? Lost your license?"

"Retired."

"You don't look older than forty."

"Thanks. Gee."

"I mean it."

"I'm thirty-eight."

"Nice," she said.

"I don't do that work anymore," I said.

"Why not?"

"I'd rather sit around on my boat," I said.

"Sounds boring," she said.

"It has its moments," I said.

"You don't have any other goals in life?" she said.

"Except for drinking and getting picked up by women I barely know in bars," I said, "no, not really."

"Are you *in*sinuating I *initiated* this?"

I raised a curious brow, not unlike Mr. Spock in *Star Trek*.

"You cocky bastard," she said, reaching over to hit me on the arm.

I shrugged.

We stood there and looked at each other, and it was a stupid moment.

"You don't know *shit* about shit," she said and quickly left me alone on my boat.

3.

My boat. I never saw myself as a boat person, and then one day I obtained some incriminating evidence on a client's estranged wife, saving him a bundle of cash and a headache on the divorce settlement. Along with giving me a hefty bonus, he said, "How would you like a boat? It's not a yacht or anything, but it's cozy and could be fun and I don't need it; I'd like you to have it." I said why not and figured I could always sell it. The boat sat in the marina docks under my name, the mooring fee coming out of my checking account each month, for nearly three years. I let friends from out of town or having domestic problems stay on it now and then, but for the most part it sat there on the waterfront, empty. Every month I kept telling myself to put an ad in the paper and get rid of it but I always seemed to forget; perhaps subconsciously I didn't want to get rid of it. Which, it seems, was a good thing. My life was quiet and uneventful until that night I fucked Erin. I was no longer interested in excitement, adventure, sordidness, and crime after I took three .38 slugs in the gut during a really stupid case, was in the hospital for three months, was told over and over, "It's a miracle you're still alive." So I quit the private-eye biz and moved onto this boat, living on savings and taking my time deciding what the next career would be.

4.

I was sitting in the Yacht Club on my second vodka tonic when Erin sat down across from me with a robust fellow in his fifties, who had a bald head, a great tan, a white beard, and a white sports coat with blue slacks.

"Erin," I said.

"I'd like you to meet my husband, Bobby," she said.

The man shook my hand and his grip was tight, but there didn't seem to be any anger in either his grip or his eyes. "Erin told me all about you," he said.

"Did she now," I said.

But he was quite friendly with me: "How you used to be a bonafide shamus! That's really great. Always wish I'd done something like that."

"Always wished I'd been a brain surgeon," I mumbled, not really in the mood to be too much of a smart ass tonight.

"Anyway, I saw you sitting there and I told Bobby-boo," said Erin, "I told Bobbob, 'Let's invite him to our party this weekend.'"

"Indeed," said Bobby-boo, "we'd love to have you as a guest."

"It'll be fun," Erin said, kicking me under the table with her pointed toe.

Her tap hurt. I didn't let it show.

"Sure," I said, "I'd love to."

5.

I'd love to, my ass. But what do you say when you're talking to the husband of a woman who, just a week earlier, had squirted her fuck juice straight down your throat?

Still, Saturday night came, I had nothing to do, I didn't feel like sitting around on my little boat, so I put on a dress shirt and my nice leather sports coat and walked up several docking piers to Erin and Bobby's large boat, dubbed *The Sympathy*. It was a giant, bright white beauty made by Crescent

Custom: seven cabins, a large entertainment area, a sailboat the size of mine attached to the back. There was a hot tub with several naked people drinking wine in it. The party seemed several hours underway. Loud contemporary jazz played on the sound system—something atmospheric with an upright bass and piano. Many of the attendees were fellow boat people whom I'd seen around but didn't really know. Hell, let's face it, I didn't know anybody and I didn't know squat, which was always the problem with me and is why I always found myself in the shit that I seemed to easily sink into.

For instance, Stephanie . . .

6.

But first there was Erin. Holding a tall glass of champagne, she spotted me. She was wearing a low-cut, sheer green silk evening gown that was practically see-through. I wondered why she bothered wearing anything at all: I could see her nipples and the hint of pubic hair through that fine fabric. Maybe that was the point, because I instantly decided this view of her was far more erotic and enticing than if she were naked like her guests in the hot tub.

"Hey," she said, "thanks for coming." She gave me a kiss on the cheek, grabbed my hand, and said, "you look good." Then she moved her mouth close to my ear and whispered, "maybe later we can slip away for some quick fun." She took a step back and said, "Have fun. Get yourself a drink, why don't you."

I started making my way toward the bar when Bobby intercepted me like we were on a basketball court. "Mr. Private Eyeball!" he said and chuckled, first grabbing me by the shoulders and then vigorously shaking my hand. "Good to see you here! Having fun? Oh, you don't have a drink. Go make yourself a drink this instant, fellow!"

At the bar, I started to make myself a tall White Russian. A young woman appeared at my side. She didn't look any older than twenty, but what did I know. She could have been fifteen or thirty, I could no longer tell. She was wearing a pink halter top and a very mini denim skirt. Her legs were skinny and smooth and tanned. Her arms, shoulders, and chest were just as tanned. She wasn't wearing a bra, and her nipples were dark, pointy, and yummy. Her eyes were blue and she was a blonde (of course).

"Looks good," she said, "make me one?"

I gave her mine.

"Oh," she said.

I started making another.

"Nice," she said when she sipped it.

"Most bartenders don't know how to make a White Russian for garbanzo beans," I told the girl. "A great beverage of this ilk should always be one-thirds equal parts."

"Right," she said and nodded her cute little blonde head of hair. "They usually get too thick on the milk or Kahlúa and not the vodka. Oh, by the way, I'm Stephanie," and she held out her small, smooth hand.

7.

We chitchatted, we talked, we moved about the giant yacht to places where we seemed to be alone and could talk. It doesn't matter what we talked about, and I'm not even sure I remember. We did drink a number of my specially made White Russians. Stephanie said she had to pee and excused herself but then came back and said, "The women's restroom is occupied and there's a line and I really have to go, you wouldn't mind if I . . . oh fuck it," and what she did was lifted her miniskirt, pushed her thong panties out of the way, hoisted herself up on the safety rail, and pointed her ass and crotch toward the water. She almost slipped and fell, and I caught her, and she said, "My knight in shining something," and, holding onto me, she let it fly: a long stream of piss heading straight into the marina. No one at the soiree seemed to notice, or they didn't want to notice; Stephanie found this funny, she giggled, and I guess I found it amusing as well and laughed, and the next thing I knew I was kissing her. I was kissing her as she relieved herself over the bow.

8.

And then I was in one of the cabins with Stephanie on the bed, pushing those thong panties out of the way so I could get my cock inside her tight little pussy, her legs on my shoulders, the miniskirt around her hips, one tit peeking out from the halter. "Fuck me hard," she said, "I mean *really* hard, old man," pressing her fingernails into my neck, "fuck me good, baby." I did my best.

9.

Stephanie and I were going at it a second time. She was sucking me off and helping me up for the adventure. Erin walked in on us. She leaned against the wall and said, "Isn't this *some*thing." She said, "Isn't this a *sight.*"

Stephanie popped my dick out and said in a raspy tone, "Wanna join us, you pervert?"

Erin's dress seemed to slip off her body, and she was naked and standing next to the bed. "If you don't mind, I'd like to, yes."

"Do you mind?" Stephanie asked me.

I said, "Only a fool would mind," or something like that.

I knew this was going to be a mistake but at the moment I didn't give a fuck. Or I did give a fuck—two fucks and a blow job, actually.

10.

Erin got up and she suddenly had a bottle of something and cups. Where did she get it? Who cared? I needed a drink like they did, and so we drank and eyed each other's sweaty, shiny, fuck-stinky flesh. The two women started to lip dance all over my body. After two drinks I started to feel funny. I was dizzy but as horny as a male finch in a cage with a dozen winged bitches. "You slipped me a fucking mickey," I said. The two women laughed. I giggled with them. I couldn't move from the bed. I was numb all over but my prick was thick and hard.

11.

"Now isn't *this* a sight," said Bobby as he walked in on the three of us. We all chuckled and pointed at him and told him to get naked. He got naked. It was then that I noticed he was holding a camcorder.

12.

I woke up to a bright sunny day. I felt like complete and total shit—like I had gone to Tokyo and Godzilla had stomped on me for an hour and a half. I was also naked, and my crotch and mouth smelled of dried pussy juice, and I'm sure most of it came from Erin. I found my clothes on the floor and put them on. Erin and Stephanie's clothes were there, but no Erin and Stephanie. On the deck I found Erin and Bobby sunning their bodies and drinking mimosas. Bobby wore a black Speedo, and Erin was topless with a pair of thong panties. Twenty feet away from them lay Stephanie, spread-eagle on a giant towel, completely nude and working on that wonderful tan. They all said good morning. I mumbled something. Erin asked if I wanted a mimosa and I said, "Why the hell not."

"Please sit down, my friend," Bobby said, patting a chair between him and his wife.

I sat and sipped my mimosa.

"Hair of the dog, eh?" said Bobby.

I couldn't reply. I shrugged.

"Quite a night," said Stephanie, sitting up, what little fat she had on her belly making small curls.

"Oh boy," said Bobby.

"Oh yeah," said Erin.

"Ugh," said I.

"I have something to show you," Bobby said, standing up. Did I have to see all that hair? "Please," he said, "come with me."

I followed him into the boat's entertainment center. There was a forty-two-inch plasma screen. Erin and Stephanie joined us, not bothering to cover themselves. They sat very close to each other on a loveseat. I didn't like how this was playing out but I was too hungover and enjoying the mimosa to give a damn.

I was ready for anything, I suppose, but I really wasn't ready for what happened next.

Bobby had a remote control in his left hand. He hit play. On the plasma was some low-lit porn, home porn, and I was the star; Erin and Stephanie were the starlets, except, when on-screen, they were going at each other, which caused them in real life to giggle at one another and kiss. Watching themselves was getting the two women, who looked like mother and daughter at that moment, all hot 'n' throbbin' again.

I said, "Funny."

Erin said, "Tell him."

Bobby said, "Here's the deal, gumshoe. It's time to put those ol' shoes back on and get 'em dirty again. It's time to do the voodoo that I know you do oh so very moo-moo," and he chuckled like he'd just said the funniest thing in the whole wide goddamn fucking world.

I said, "What?"

Erin said, "Tell him, BoBo."

"This," and Bobby pointed to the plasma screen that had Stephanie's lubed-up hand sliding three fingers into my asshole, "is good ol' fashioned blackmail."

"Fast forward it to the nasty stuff," Erin said.

"Yeah," Stephanie said, playing with Erin's nipples, *"the nasty!"*

Bobby hit fast forward to the part where Stephanie and I were in the bathroom taking turns pissing in each other's mouths.

"Nothing like a little golden shower between complete strangers," Bobby said.

Hmm. I even remembered that part.

13.

"So what's the deal?" I asked.

"Here's the deal," Bobby said. "There's a fellow two piers down, who has a really huge yacht, *The Sherri Love.* His name is Roland Wilson. Do you know him?"

"No," I said, "but I've seen the boat."

"He's an *ass*hole," Erin said.

"Yes, a real ass*hole,"* said Bobby, "and something needs to be done about him."

"What does that have to do with me and this?" I asked.

Now, on the plasma screen, I was making Stephanie lick my balls.

"Wilson is clean, *too* clean on paper. I need some *dirt* on him. Something very, very bad. It'll have to be planted."

"And just exactly where and when do I come into the picture?"

"You'll plant the bad shit! And it has to be bad enough to ruin his reputation, maybe even make his wife leave him and his children disown his ass."

"And what makes you think I can help you with this evil plan?"

I polished off the mimosa and wanted to ask for another but knew well enough not to.

"You're in that kind of business, buddy," he said.

I laughed.

"We did some checking around."

"We asked questions," Erin chimed in, proudly.

"We found out you didn't exactly move by the playbook for private eyes."

"You have your skeletons."

"Who doesn't," I said and looked at Stephanie: "And where do you come into all of this?"

"She's just the hired gun," Bobby said.

"More like *hired pussy,*" Stephanie said, opening her legs and touching herself.

"And a nice one at that," Bobby observed.

"I'll say," Erin did say, running her hand across the pussy in question.

"And I don't come cheap," Stephanie added.

"We got our money's worth," Erin said.

"I think I'll be going now," I said.

"No," Bobby said, "you will sit down and listen."

14.

"If you don't do what we want, we'll spread this tape around and ruin your life."

Well. I had a really good laugh.

I said, "Go ahead. I don't *have* a reputation or life to destroy. That was done long ago. You picked the wrong washed-out alcoholic man for sexual extortion. I don't have a career, family, or even any personal integrity to jeopardize. So send the tape anywhere you want. Hell, who knows, maybe I'll get laid more often."

"I doubt it," said Erin, "you're a drunk and not so good in bed."

"Look who's talking, Lady Leaky Faucet."

She made a face: *ha-ha.*

"Stephanie is young and looks even younger," Bobby said, "we could send the tape to the cops and tell them she's fifteen."

"I'm only in high school and this bad old man seduced me," said Stephanie in a funny small voice, like Japanese anime; she was sucking on her thumb and batting her eyelashes, too. It was a damn good acting job, I thought.

"But you're not," I said.

"It'll still cause you trouble," Erin said.

I shrugged. "I can take some trouble."

"There's something else," Bobby said, "and that's Stephanie's boyfriend."

"He's a big, jealous, mean killing machine," said Stephanie, "and let me tell you, boy, if he ever got a gander of that vid-vid, he'd hunt you down, skin you alive, and then barbecue your hide and feed it to the bikers who go to the bar that he owns."

"I've seen him," Erin told me, nodding her head, "and he *is* big and mean."

"And my oh my quite *ugly,*" Stephanie went on, "but I love him so."

"He knows you're a whore?" I said.

"He loves whores."

"Well," I said, taking in a deep breath.

"So what will it be, gumshoe?" asked Bobby.

"My answer," I told the three of them, "is for you to all go fuck off and die. Do whatever you want. Break a bunch of legs. *Bonne chance*, like the French say. As for me, I say: 'Fuck you very much.'"

I got up and started to walk away. I expected someone to pull a gun on me, but there was no gun.

Before I parted ways with this trio of criminal misfits, I stopped and said, "Assholes."

"You'll regret this," Bobby said.

"Probably," I said.

15.

Returned to my boat and sobered up by drinking bottled Fiji water for most of the day and getting more sleep. Fiji water usually does the trick. I took a nap and dreamt that I sailed my boat to Fiji where I lived peacefully and happily ever after. Night came, and I wondered what Bobby and Erin would actually do. I got dressed and decided to pay a visit to *The Sherri*

Love. Jesus, that was one big boat; it was an Italian-made Benetti Patricia class. Twenty cabins—an apartment building on water. Must've cost ten or fifteen million. I called up, I said I needed to speak to Roland Wilson. I said it was very important. I was let aboard. Roland Wilson was a man in his mid-fifties, very well built and wearing all black: slacks, T-shirt, sports coat, loafers. He had a long, gray beard. I'd heard he'd made his fortune in some sort of biotech stock deal. I met him in the dining area of the boat. He was having rib-eye steak, which smelled like heaven. I was offered dinner but I declined. At his side was a woman in her early twenties, a brunette with saucer-shaped eyes and a soft, white body, like she hardly went out in the sun—odd for a boat person.

"This is my wife, Sherri," Wilson said. *The boat!*

"Nice to meet you," I said.

"Likewise," she said, very softly.

"To what do I owe the pleasure of your visit?" asked Roland Wilson. "Your face is familiar, but we've never met."

"It ain't good news," I said.

"I'm assuming it's not."

So I told him everything—well, not everything, but enough.

"I see," Wilson said. "Well, I'm not surprised."

"He's a bastard," said Sherri.

"So there's some bad blood," I said.

"You can say that," Wilson said. "I married his daughter, Sherri, for one. He was not happy about that. The age difference, of course. I married her the day she turned eighteen, although we'd been carrying on since she was . . ."

"Roland," said his wife, *"please."*

"Her first job was at a certain pharmaceutical company. Some information came her way, she passed it along to me, and I turned my life's savings into a fortune. What she did not do, however, was share these trade secrets with her father and his wife, her stepmother. They tried to get the SEC to investigate, but there simply was no hard evidence. Since the statute of limitations has since run out, we can freely admit our little insider-trading scheme. You do what you have to do . . . to get ahead in this world. Wouldn't you say so?"

"Sure," I said, and to Sherri: "Erin is your stepmom?"

"Do you *know* the *cunt?*"

"Language, dear," said her husband, patting her bare knee.

"I mean 'bitch.'"

I said, "We've met."

"She hates me. I hate her. It's a simple story."

"I don't get it," I said, "you all live in the same marina?"

"We were here first," Wilson said. "Sherri's father made some money doing what he did, day trading and that sort of thing, and he and his wife purchased a boat and specifically moved here."

"To make our lives unpleasant," Sherri said.

"Why not move?" I asked.

"Why give them the satisfaction?" Wilson said.

"They're pretty bent on ruining you."

"They can try. I appreciate your coming to me with this."

"Why not. They tried to blackmail me."

"What do I owe you for this information?"

"Nothing."

"Oh, please."

"Well."

"Name your price."

"Like?"

"Name it."

"Five grand," I said.

"Let me write you a check," he said.

16.

Check in pocket and feeling pretty damn dandy about being paid for my good deed of the day, I walked back to my tiny boat. I didn't make it. I was jumped by two big guys with lousy intentions. One held me still while another knocked me on the back of the head with something quite hard and cold.

17.

The headache I had when I woke up was worse than the morning's hangover. I felt a lump that had dried blood on it. I was lying on a smelly, old green army cot in a narrow room filled with empty beer kegs and boxes of hard booze. A large man, his muscles going to fat, sat across from me in a white lawn chair. He had a thin moustache and long hair, and I had a feeling he may have been the fellow who gave me the headache. I owed him one.

"Where am I?" I asked.

"Hey, Gregory!" the man said to the closed door.

The door opened, and another big man (whose fat seemed

to be turning into muscles, like he'd just discovered the world of weightlifting three months ago) walked in. He was bald. I figured he was the one I had to settle with—I noticed a black revolver tucked into his pants. There was loud music and cheering coming from somewhere in the building. The place smelled like stale booze, piss, and cheap disinfectant mixed with bleach.

"Get a good nap?" he said with a grin.

"You're Gregory?"

"And this is Steve. Steve, go get Tony."

The other man stood and left. Gregory sat in the lawn chair. I didn't think that poor piece of plastic would hold out much longer, the way it bent and made strange sounds that no lawn chair should ever make.

"So what's the story," I said, "Gregory."

"You fucked up, pal."

"No kidding."

"Tony is pissed."

"Who is Tony?"

"*I'm* Tony, *motherfucker,*" said the man who walked in, followed by Steve. He was around six foot five, skinny, tattooed, with long black hair in a ponytail. He wore leather pants, cowboy boots, and a vest. He would've been handsome if his face weren't so pockmarked. He tossed something at me, and I caught it. It was a videocassette. "I watched your movie," he said.

"Oh shit," I said.

"'Oh shit' is right."

"I take it you're Stephanie's boyfriend?"

She said he was ugly and she wasn't kidding.

"Why must we resort to labels and expectations? The cunt is my property. What I want to know is what were you doing fucking what is mine when you didn't get my permission or even pay for it?"

With that, he came over to me and backhanded me across the face. I tasted blood. I rubbed my jaw.

"I was set up."

All three of them laughed.

I said, "Really."

"Tell me about it."

So I did.

The three of them looked at each other.

"That's so nutty I believe it," Tony said. "Fuck it," he said, "I'm sick of this bullshit. Go get Nancy," he told Gregory, and Gregory nodded and left.

"Why am I here?"

"To rough your shit up, maybe even kill you, but now I see you're just a fucking dupe. Like Homer Simpson in *The Day of the Locust*. Ever see that movie? One of my faves. Donald Sutherland was great in it. So you got caught up in the pussy game. Happens to the best of us, but mostly happens to the worst, y'know. She used to get me, Steph did. She used to get me to do what she wanted; get me all pissed off and hurt any man she had a problem with. But you know what? This is the last time. This is it. I'm not playing anymore. This time she's going down into the sea and sleeping with the fishes, like they say in the gangster movies. This time she's dug her own grave. I'm officially breaking up with her."

Gregory returned with a redhead in gold high heels and black panties and bra. She could have been twenty, she could have been forty. She looked tired.

Tony said, "This is Nancy. She's my apology to you. So have your bad ol' self some fun and then I'll see to it you get back home."

I was left alone with the woman.

"You okay?" she said.

"Yeah," I said.

She sat next to me. "You sure you're okay?"

I said, "Yeah."

She smelled like cheap wine and baby powder.

She said, "You want to kiss me?"

"Do I have to?"

"You should," and she leaned in to kiss my cheek and whispered: "You won't be okay soon. You're in danger."

"How?"

"Mmm, baby, that's good," she said loudly, for effect, then whispered: "We don't have to do this. I don't want to do this. I don't like seeing people get hurt, especially stupid men like you."

"I don't like seeing myself get hurt either."

"I don't want to do this," and she added loudly: "Yeah, baby, touch me right there like that!"

"What the fuck," I said.

She whispered: "They always set up poor saps like you, and use me to do it. We start fucking, then Tony's goons come up and smack you around, just when you're about to get your rocks off, and leave you broken and bloody and naked in the street for the cops to find. It's not pretty, let me tell you, and I bet it's embarrassing as hell."

"Great."

"But that doesn't have to happen."

"It won't," I said. "Just keep up your act."

She started to moan and say nasty, sexy things. I grabbed one of the empty beer kegs and moved it next to the door. I nodded to Nancy. She yelled, "Oh yeah baby, fuck me deep!" A few seconds later the door opened and Steve came in. I picked up the empty keg and brought it down on his head. He went to the floor, unconscious. I reached for one of the booze boxes and yanked out a fifth of Jose Cuervo Gold. Gregory burst in next like an elephant out of the jungle. I smashed the bottle across his face and rammed the jagged end into his belly. He went to his knees, cursing my existence like a mad Catholic priest. I relieved him of his gun.

"I'll be going now," I said.

"You'll be going to hell," he said.

"I already have," I said.

18.

I escaped out the back exit. There were a lot of motorcycles and hot rods parked outside the building, a placed called Tony Hole with a neon sign: LIVE NUDE WOMEN AND GIRLS. I was somewhere in Mission Beach from the looks of it. Not too far from home. I found a parked taxi and told the driver to take me downtown. It was a good thing I had a few bills in my wallet. I still had my check from Roland Wilson too. I couldn't wait to get to my boat, curl up in bed, and pretend the last two days never happened. But I wasn't going to find peace on the calm waters of the marina boat docks. There were a dozen Harbor Patrol police cars and two ambulances, and they seemed to be focused on *The Sherri Love*. I saw Sherri Wilson, a blanket covering her shoulders, talking to three police officers. I didn't want to know what was going on. I did my best to keep away from the cops, since I had a gun on me and my face and head were bloodied up.

19.

There was someone in my boat, sitting on my bed.

"It's good to see you," Stephanie said. She was wearing cut-off shorts and a tank top and had no shoes.

"I can't say the same. You're not welcome here."

"Oh please," she said, standing and coming to me. She tried to cuddle, she tried to kiss. I pushed her away. "Do you hate me so?" she asked like a little girl to a bad daddy.

"I just got away from Tony."

"I'm sorry. Things didn't work out as planned."

"What? That Tony didn't kill me or make me a cripple?"

"If it makes you feel better, he wants to break my arms and legs too, and this time he means it. That's why I gotta lay low. I gotta hide, I gotta run away. And because of what's going on out there . . . "

"What *is* going on out there?"

"Bobby snapped and took a shotgun to kill Roland Wilson. But Wilson was ready and shot Bobby. So Erin snapped and went after Wilson with a huge knife, and Wilson shot her, too. They're both dead."

"It was self-defense."

I hoped so, anyway. I wondered if my check would clear. Then again, I'm sure Wilson could hire the best lawyers to iron it all out. I hoped I wouldn't have to testify. I hoped the porn tape wouldn't have to be played in court.

Stephanie said, "I don't know why I got caught up in all this."

"Money."

"Um-hm."

"Everything we do . . . we do for money."

"Or love," she said, "and hate."

She said she couldn't leave, she was afraid. She cried, and my heart went soft—just a little. She asked to sleep here with me. She said I could have her; I could do anything I wanted as long as I didn't send her out there to the wolves.

We went to bed.

I flipped her onto her stomach and pulled her shorts down. I said, "Bad girls get it up the ass."

"I am bad and I want it that way," she said, "yes, give it to me that way, that's what I want and deserve."

Sure, I was going to do it, but not right away. I wanted to have a little fun first—call it a going-away present. I was sober this time, I was more aware, I was able to enjoy this young woman's body. I ran my tongue along every part of her lithe, tanned body, from her forehead to her toes, because I knew this would probably be the one and last time I would have the opportunity to taste such an exquisitely naughty nymph. *Carpe diem*, as the old saying goes, and I did plenty of carpe. When I got between her legs and clamped my hungry mouth on her dirty little pussy, I hoped she would squirt like Erin, I hoped I would get a full acidic taste of Stephanie, but not much luck—when she came, she came just like any other woman: with a small shriek, a shudder, and the digging of her nails into my back.

She didn't draw blood.

I wished she would. I deserved to bleed.

Instead, I drew blood from her. I moved up and took her left, hard nipple into my mouth and bit down.

"Owie-wowie," she said, and sighed, and said, "Bite me harder, Mr. Private Eyeball."

And so I did, and I tasted her blood, and her blood made my cock get very hard.

This is when I flipped her on her stomach and shoved it in her hot little waiting ass.

"Do I get punished now?" she asked.

I said, "This is only the beginning, baby."

Her asshole was burning and juicy and took me in like a wife welcoming her soldier home from war.

20.

When she fell asleep, I made a phone call.

21.

Met him at the entrance of the pier. I had Gregory's revolver pointed at his heart.

"You're alone?" I asked.

"I said I'd come alone, like we agreed."

"You got the money?"

"Right here."

He tossed over a wad of bills: $2,000, as agreed.

I handed him the gun. "It's not loaded anymore."

Tony smiled. "No hard feelings. Gregory had an ass-whoopin' coming to him. And because you made that call, we're even, and you have a few extra dollars in your pocket. Where is she?"

"Asleep on my boat. But whatever you do, do it somewhere else. Not on my sail ride. Do it far away."

"I like you, brother. You're a cold-hearted bastard. We're cut from the same cloth."

"Payback sucks," I said.

"It's a bitch, all right," he said.

"Yeah," I said, walking away.

"Hey, Nancy tells me you're a *great* fuck!"

"Yeah," I said.

He laughed, and I did not.

OUT OF THE CLOSET

Bill Noble

I tilt my watch to catch the pink glow of a streetlamp half a block away. When it flicks over to 9:00, I drift toward the leafy entryway of 47 Crestwood Drive and, in the embrace of the soft California night, nudge the front door; already unlatched, it swings silently open. I slip inside.

In near darkness, broad, carpeted stairs curve up and out of sight. I tiptoe upward a few steps, listen, and climb again.

Upstairs, Debbie and Val's easy, intimate murmuring filters through the bathroom door in counterpoint to the splash of water. *The bubble bath—right on schedule.* Cat-footed, I move toward the open door at the end of the hall: Val's room. Candlelight flickers on its walls.

The bed lies open, waiting.

I have instructions. But when I try to slide the closet door open, its rollers rumble ominously. The closet shares a wall with the bathroom: I can hear the smallest splash and teasing word from the two women on its other side. I coax the door a fraction of an inch at a time, freezing at every sound until water begins to run again in the tub; with that as cover I push the door a last few inches and squeeze inside.

I slide the door closed again, leaving a gap that gives me a view of the bed. Overhead, dresses and coats have been pushed aside; a chair huddles in the small open space that's been created. I smile: *Of course she'd have everything ready for me. Debbie's been obsessing over this for weeks.* I peel off my clothes and fold them in a pile on the floor. I slip condoms and lube out of my daypack. The chair creaks in protest as I ease onto it, so I stand again, head craned painfully forward to avoid banging the clothes pole. But I make sure I'm still able to watch the bed. Naked in the dark, I wait. And wait. The sounds of bathing, sensual and unhurried, go on and on. It's forty minutes before I hear two bodies emerge dripping from the bath on the other side of the wall.

Val pads into the bedroom first. In the candlelight her beauty is overpowering: smooth, ivory-white, nearly six feet tall, with a swimmer's unconscious grace; great, dark innocent eyes; a seallike sleekness. She tends the candles, drops her towel, and stands quietly by the bed, waiting.

Debbie follows, small, lean, and keen of eye, every muscle mobile under dark-gold skin, towel dangling from one hand. I glimpse the paired lips of her sex as she bends; my cock stirs. She doesn't so much as glance toward the closet. I've known this woman's steely will for more than a few years: nothing will distract her from her plan.

She perches on the bed and, by accident or design, pulls Val around to face her, positioned perfectly for me to watch. Val bends and puts her mouth over Debbie's, but after a lingering kiss Debbie pulls away. "I think it's gonna be a leather and chain night," Debbie says, smiling a challenge. "Dress for me."

Val hesitates a moment, then turns and pulls tangled paraphernalia from a dresser drawer. Facing Debbie, she straps her torso with black leather and chrome chain that isolates and exaggerates her full breasts. The harness she buckles tight around her hips and pulls tight through her crotch does the same for her pale haunches. She cinches a broad collar, stiff and constricting, around her long neck. Debbie sprawls on the bed, a single finger tolling between her legs. Not a word is spoken.

In the cramped closet, an unrelenting ache pulses the length of my cock; I struggle to keep my hand away from the ache.

Val kneels. Debbie dangles the cold chain of a leash over Val's breasts until I see gooseflesh rise. Tension. Resistance. They stare into one another's eyes for a long time. Debbie produces a blindfold. Val's eyes flash, but after a moment she drops her gaze and puts it on.

"Pleasure me."

Debbie's voice doesn't invite discussion. Val gropes for her, parts her legs, buries her face between them. Her leather-blind eyes peer up toward Debbie's face. Not six feet from me, two beautiful women make love in candlelight. Val's white face mouths and pushes, serving Debbie's pleasure. Debbie's brown body arches and pants. Every small sound wrenches my arousal tighter, until my hand gropes for my cock of its own volition. I grab it and squeeze viciously. *God, don't let me come!*

Val licks. Debbie, straining and panting, wrenches herself back from the brink of orgasm again and again; I can't tell, ultimately, if she lets herself go over the edge or not. I strain to hold my hand motionless. *Only a woman could endure so much pleasure.*

"Stop."

Val draws back, the black leather of the blindfold half hiding her dripping face.

"Lie down."

Val stretches herself on the sheets, face up, undefended. Debbie comes to the closet, slides back the door, and waves me wordlessly to a folded futon at the foot of the bed.

She strips off Val's harness, top and bottom, and begins to stroke her. Fingertips, the barest touch. Val's body opens, her mouth slack, her breasts rising, her pelvis twisting slowly under the half-withheld pleasuring. The long muscles in her thighs knot and release. A long, mewling plea spirals out of her; a rush of pre-cum floods my cock.

Beyond resisting, I stroke myself. Slow. Fast. Slow again. I pump till every muscle in my body locks and strains. I bring myself right to the edge—and pull back, spasming. I feather-finger my balls. I caress my belly, run fingernails down the insides of my thighs. I circle the head of my cock with my own wetness until my whole body vibrates—and all the time I don't let a single sound escape my lips: no groan, no ragged breath, nothing. I lever myself half-upright to display my hardness for Debbie, but in the hour that drifts by, playing Val's body with a relentless ferocity that is deliberately just short of enough to let Val come, she never looks directly at me. She'll confess later that she didn't dare, that her whole being was locked on keeping herself slow and in control.

Val begins to babble, but Debbie quiets her. She continues the implacable, tender arousal. When she finally ceases touching Val's body, it continues to undulate in the same steady rhythm as before, her mouth twisted in a grimace of sensation.

"Val?"

Val sighs.

"I need to tell you, hon. We're not alone. There's a man in the room. He's been watching us and stroking his cock this whole time."

Val tightens. Then she relaxes and laughs. "You're always such a mindfucker. Why should I expect anything different tonight?"

"No. He hid in the closet while we were taking our bath. I let him out after you put the blindfold on, and now he's right here at the foot of the bed."

"Are you telling the truth?" Val's voice quavers.

"Would you rather believe he's *not* here?"

Val slumps, edgy but confused, caught between panic and denial. "Debbie, tell me the truth." She's begging.

Debbie moves away from the bed.

"Deb?"

No response.

"Debbie?" Val's voice holds a razor-edge of terror. "Debbie, if anybody else's hand touches me, I'm going to freak. I don't want to play this game."

Debbie comes back to the bed and launches into easy, reassuring play. The two of them snuggle side by side; Val relaxes again into her partner's love.

Beneath the blindfold, Val smiles. "Y'know, you didn't have to stop that story. I was kinda liking it."

Debbie's grin spreads. "That's nice, hon, because it's true. He's right there, pumping his hard, red cock, ready to do anything I tell him."

"Shit, Debbie." A little, lost-girl voice is all Val can summon.

Debbie climbs off the bed again and waits in silence. I watch Val's body. It recoils from imaginary touches, flinches at the tiniest current of air.

Debbie waits.

After a long time, she motions to me to stand and to put my hands around Val's ankles. My cock flaps clumsily as I bend over the bed. I grip her with all the tenderness I can manage, trying not to tremble. Val stiffens, then relaxes, apparently deciding it's Debbie touching her.

Debbie climbs onto the foot of the bed. Inch by inch, she slides up Val's body. When she's stretched nearly full-length beside her, sudden understanding shudders through Val's flesh: the hands around her ankles cannot possibly be Debbie's.

I tighten my grip in the same moment. She screams.

It's a piercing, whole-body scream. She convulses in my grasp, knots herself into a tight fetal position. She's shaking from head to foot.

"Payback time for that scene you created last month, Val. You're *my* toy tonight, hon." Then Debbie rocks Val in her arms to soothe her.

Val whispers into the curve of Debbie's neck. "Suppose I take the blindfold off?"

"The game ends."

Val lies curled on the bed. Debbie strokes her. Without warning, Val throws herself across Debbie full-force and jams her fingers into Debbie's pussy. She's overwhelmingly bigger and stronger—there's no possibility of resistance. Val finger-fucks her. Hard. Debbie fights until sensation overwhelms her, then her body arches off the bed. She shouts, once, and a stream of clear liquid spurts onto her thighs and sprays the sheets.

She collapses.

Somehow, I'm still holding Val's ankles, watching this strange power struggle play itself out, feeling the ferocity of it.

Debbie's breathing returns gradually to normal. Val, still blindfolded, looks utterly at peace now, curled up beside her. Minutes tick by in silence.

"That was nice, Val." Debbie is whispering. "So nice I may even let this guy fuck you . . . later." Debbie struggles upright. She looks at me, appraisingly, then back at Val. "Kneel."

Uncertain, Val maneuvers herself off the bed to kneel upright on the rug. My whole body is a bomb ready to explode, my cock the white-hot fuse. My balls are cramped so tight they hurt. My arousal has been so prolonged that my cock has darkened to a leaden purple.

Debbie summons me with a gesture. I come and stand in front of Val, my straining cock an inch from her mouth, torn between compassion and lust.

"Suck him." Debbie's voice is throaty, urgent.

Val begins a blind search. When she finds me, she slides her lips along my length, nuzzling my pubic hair, playing, holding back. Her face is undefended, vulnerable—but the slightest ghost of a smile catches at the corner of her mouth. *Suck me. I know how much you like sucking me. Suck me, for Christ's sake!*

She licks up the underside of me. Her tongue curls to catch a drop of pre-cum and then swirls over and around the top. My hips jut forward, pleading, and she lets the tip of me slip into her mouth. Grinning, she licks and lips and sucks until I can't keep my hips from jittery thrusts. But I'm a hired cock tonight—the whole scene depends on my shadowy anonymity, on Val having no idea who I am—I can't make a sound. I groan and holler through any everyday lovemaking, and here I have to hold myself in breathless silence.

Debbie spreads herself on the bed with a vibrator, her eyes devouring us. I try to watch as she fucks herself, writhing and gulping air, but I can't look away from Val's masked face. From my swollen cock, sluiced in her mouth.

———————————

Val pulls in a deep breath and, gaping, lunges forward. Her face slams my stomach. Whatever it is Val does with her throat when she does that, I know men who'd pay millions for it.

Debbie growls: "Grab her! Fuck her face!"

I knot both hands in Val's hair and thrust. She looks as if she's been seized by religious ecstasy. I throw my whole body into fucking, driving my blunt cock again and again against the back of her throat, and she takes it, takes it all. She rakes my hips with her fingernails. Sounds jerk out of her—animal grunts and strangled whines and half-suffocated, throat-stuffed shouts that vibrate up the core of my cock. At the edge of vision I see Debbie burst into a tremendous thrashing come, and my body rushes to join her climax, to catapult itself over the edge . . .

"Stop!"

"Now!"

I have no idea if Debbie's bellow is aimed at Val or at me, but both of us slow. I'm teetering over the abyss, flailing, trying to haul myself back from orgasm. *Fucking bitch!* In a red flash, I understand that Debbie is dominating *me,* too. That she's getting off on it, big time.

Val groans.

Debbie waves me away and pulls Val on top of her. "Good little slut," she says, syrupy.

"Debbie, you bitch! You can't stop now. He hasn't fucked me!"

Val looks possessed. Her ass is undulating, aimed straight toward me. Her shining swollen cunt gapes and pulses.

Over Val's back, Debbie makes a single stubbed gesture with her fist. *Fuck her.*

In a single step, I'm at the closet, rolling a condom onto a cock as heavy and awkward as a baseball bat. Back at the bed, Debbie pulls Val up so their sodden, slippery clits are smeared together, Val on top. A foot and a half of crotch—Val's and Debbie's stacked together—waits for me, dark, soaking, fertile.

I kneel between their legs. With one hand, I press my cock head against Val's opening. The muscles along her spine ridge.

I brace my arms along Debbie's rib cage, looking down into her face. Repeating the words *slow . . . slow . . . slow* silently like a prayer, I let my cock cantilever forward to fill Val. I'm pressed, sweating, pulse pounding, against her from the nape of her neck to the taut soles of her feet.

I arch. I thrust again. I feel through the skin of my scrotum the weight of my body forcing their clits together. I withdraw, and thrust. Again. Again. Slow. Slow.

Val and Debbie kiss, if you can use the word "kiss" for something so carnivorous. Debbie's breath scalds my face, our three gaping mouths inches apart. Sweat fills the sucking gap between my belly and the small of Val's back. That sound goads the three of us toward even greater intensity. Again. Again. *Jesus God.* Again.

Our bodies find a single music. Muscle. Cock. Cunt. Woman. Man.

Us.

We come.

How much time has passed I can't tell. I lie tangled with these two long-familiar bodies, immersed in the mingled scents and the soft sounds of our breathing. Debbie's fingers stray to smooth the hair along my temple, and I remember just that touch from nights past—from the years before she dived with such abandon into women, before she and Val wrestled and fucked and provoked and dared their way into this fiery tug-of-war relationship they've invented.

Debbie aims a lazy, replete smile at me, but her words are for Val, sprawled face up beside her. "Would you like to take the blindfold off?"

Val tugs it up over her head, unsnarls it from her hair, and drops it to the floor. It takes a moment for her eyes to focus, and then she sees me. "Dan." It's barely a whisper. And then tears flood her cheeks. "Oh, Danny, Danny." I was Val's lover, too, once a long time ago, but we haven't veered toward intimacy in all the time since she and Debbie have been together—until tonight. And now I'm invited back, fully back, even if just for the night.

I kiss her.

I kiss Debbie.

They kiss back, kiss each other, keep kissing until our kissing becomes a sort of prayer, a floating, wordless meditation on mouths and fingertips and shoulders and breasts and dreamy half-shuttered eyes.

One by one, the tall candles burn down, drip away, flicker, gutter out. Darkness takes the room.

We sleep.

SEE YOU DOWN THERE

Steve Almond

Back then, in Myrtle Beach, we worked out every day, two hours of lifting, one of cardio, then down to the shore to fry. We were bodybuilders, serious amateurs maybe turning pro. Rankin had won a competition out in California, in the heavy division. I was smaller but had better definition. At the gym they called me "The Chart" because you could see every muscle group. We walked around town half-naked, with our dicks hanging out. We were big and hard and our veins glistened. We wanted everyone to see.

Rankin lived with his girlfriend, Dana, who stripped at the Trap Door, and her daughter, Crystal. They had a little split level right on the beach. Dana was in her thirties. She was half Swedish, half saline—that was how she put it. Crystal was about nine. Rankin and I were both twenty-three. By April, I'd moved into their place. I slept in the Florida room, the sea breeze rolling through all night, salting my skin.

Dana didn't mind. She liked having men around, a pair of beautiful young guys. It flattered her. She knew this was some kind of arrangement. She probably even knew that Rankin kept fucking her friends, the other strippers who came by and sunbathed naked on the deck. She wasn't exactly looking for someone to grow old with.

The night I'm thinking of was mid-July, those thick days after the fourth, when the real heat settles in and the only sounds are the night dogs panting and the whistle-pop of leftover fireworks. Rankin and I headed over to the Spanish Galleon to see what the cat dragged in. Nothing. Nothing but us sausages, so we started back. Just as we got to Dana's place, an old Buick pulled up alongside of us. The window scrolled down and this little blonde said, "Where's the party, guys?"

Rankin looked at me and I looked back at him.

"Our house?" he said, hopefully.

"Groovy!" this little blonde said. "Hop in and we'll give y'all a ride." She had one of those slow Southern accents, like she was speaking through marshmallow syrup and wasn't it all, every word, just delicious?

"Actually, we live right here," Rankin said.

"Where?"

"Right here. This house." He pointed.

"How convenient," she said. "Can we park around here?"

"Wherever you please," he said. They pulled the car onto

the side of the road and hopped out. The blonde was the main attraction. Her friend was the bring-along: tall, a little gawky, with dark hair and a bump on her nose. The blonde went around to the trunk. She wore white shorts, a tank top, cowboy boots.

"What's in there?" Rankin said.

"Supplies." She popped the lock and there it was: beer in a cooler, a couple of bottles, a bag of weed, chips, ice, the works. "Always come prepared."

"Just like the Boy Scouts," Rankin said.

"That's right," the blond said. "That's us. Real *Boy Scouts*."

Rankin lifted the cooler, and the blond set her hand on his arm and made a purring noise. We ushered the girls into the living room and took their drink orders. They both wanted bourbon and Coke. I followed him into the kitchen. He turned suddenly and brought his face close to mine. "Can you believe what's happening here?"

I shook my head.

Dana was working at the Trap. She wouldn't be home till close to dawn. Crystal was staying at a friend's.

"These girls are here to get fucked tonight," Rankin said. "There is positively no doubt about that. Fucked." You couldn't have wiped the grin off his face with an atom bomb.

I'd met Rankin at the gym. We were the only two serious grinders in that place. Both of us were doing cycles. There's all this noise about steroids today, like the stuff is going to dust you if you look at it twice. But the amount we did was just perfect: enough to turn us into bulls without shrinking our nuts. Our bodies were our dreams. We wanted nice dreams.

Rankin carried the drinks into the living room and we did introductions. The blonde called herself Betty. The brunette was Veronica. We understood these to be joke names, and we couldn't have cared less. They were drinking bourbon and draping their bare legs over the furniture. These were the important facts.

They were from Fayetteville, I think. Maybe they went to school somewhere, studying something. Maybe it was interesting. We had things in common. Whatever it was. Rankin and I kept popping up to refresh the drinks. We mixed just enough soda in to keep the girls swilling. I was sitting next to Rankin on the couch. We were facing Betty, who was sitting in the recliner, with her legs falling open. Her shorts were tight denim. We could see everything.

Rankin punched my leg. "Would you look at that?" he said.

"I'm looking."

"Does that look sweet to you?"

"It does."

Betty laughed.

"That is one sweet-looking thang," Rankin said. He was imitating her accent now.

"You have *no* idea," Betty said.

"I'll bet you that tastes just like honey, J."

"I'm sure you'd like to find out," Betty said.

Rankin made a growling sound.

Veronica shook her head.

"What?" Rankin said. "What?"

"You're so porno," she said.

"I'll take that as a compliment," Rankin said.

"You would," said Veronica.

Rankin hit her with a grin. He could afford to. Little Betty was already half-gone to the booze. She'd lit up a joint, too. Everyone could see where this was headed. And really, it went this way so often. There were so many women around that summer. They came for the weekend, in rental cars, on chartered buses, to escape from their landlocked lives, their offices, their boyfriends, to break the rules, their own rules, to have something to talk about when it was over, to get tan and get drunk and get laid, and that's where Rankin and I did our work. We were friendly and uncomplicated. We knew how to flirt, how not to care too much, how to separate the ones who were willing from the ones who were serious. How to say what had to be said to a girl, at a particular moment, to bring the next moment into being, and how to make promises that could be believed just long enough to get her out of town again. It's not that we were shallow, exactly. We just had better things to do with our energies than gaze inward.

It was quite a deal we had going, between the tourists and the girls from the Trap Door, to whom we were like little brothers, a welcome relief from the mouth breathers who stared at them in sullen trances and tucked money into their garters, men immobilized by their own desperation, fat, gassy, balding, trapped in the bad dream of dwindling lives.

Another round of drinks, another joint. Betty and Rankin talked tanning, tanning salons, tanning technologies, while I toiled to get Veronica to smile.

I heard Betty say, "I don't need any players in my life."

"Oh, I get it," Rankin said. "Miss Betty's looking for Mr. Right."

"More like Mr. Right Now," Veronica said.

"You're one to talk," Betty said, "with the mouth you got on you."

"What sort of mouth is that?" I said.

"Filthy," Betty said. "Impure. Un-*Christian*." She gave the last word that old Southern extra syllable.

Veronica threw a piece of ice at Betty but hit the stereo instead.

"Seriously," Rankin said to me. "Look at that sweet little pussy. Itty Bitty Miss Betty. Is that not an epic view?"

"Puss and boots," I said.

Betty got up to look at the pictures lined up on the stereo. She stopped in front of one that showed Dana dressed in a leather mini with her arm in Rankin's lap.

"Who's this?" she said.

"My sister," Rankin said.

Veronica snorted.

"She doesn't look very much like you," Betty said.

"We have different moms."

"You mean different dads?"

Rankin paused. "No. Different moms. Same dad."

"And this is her daughter?" Betty said, holding up a photo of Crystal.

"That's right," Rankin said. "That's my niece. Little Crystal."

"How sweet," Veronica said. You could tell she was a little too smart for all this. But she was drinking her way to a greater tolerance, or seemed to be trying.

"I'm not sure I believe you," Betty said.

Rankin shrugged. "I might be lying."

"Do you make it a habit to lie to your guests?"

"Just the ones I'm hoping to fuck."

Betty giggled. "You're going to hell."

"See you down there," Rankin said.

In the kitchen, Rankin leaned close and whispered: "She's gonna need a cane when I get done with her, my man."

"A wheelchair," I said.

"Electric," he said. "She's gonna have to work the thing with her mouth."

"No doubt," I said.

It was what we said to one another back then, a kind of awful rallying cry.

And a little later, things went as they usually did. Rankin came up behind Betty and pressed himself against her, all his size, all his muscles. She made a sound, stunned, pleased, and her head fell back against his chest. Rankin walked her into the bedroom he shared with Dana, just like that, from behind.

Veronica finished her drink. "And who you supposed to be, the strong, silent type?"

I shrugged.

"I know what's happening here," she said.

"Good for you," I said. I was through trying too hard. There were plenty more where she came from.

"You guys really think you're all that."

"You're welcome to leave," I said, perfectly friendly.

Veronica smiled. "Now you're going to be mean."

I sighed. "Not at all. I'm just a little bored."

"Oh really? I'm a bore?"

"So far. Yeah."

She punched my leg. "You asshole!" She tried again, but I caught her wrist and held onto it, easy enough. She seemed to like that.

I pulled her in close, till we were just a few inches apart. "Couple things can happen here," I said. "We can go upstairs and do what you came here to do, or you can keep trying to provoke me. I'd prefer to go upstairs, but I'm not going to kiss your ass about it."

"Such a tough guy," Veronica said.

"Not tough," I said. "Just don't like wasting time."

We heard Betty let out a squeal of laughter from the other room.

"Alright tough guy," Veronica said. She took me by the hand and led me up the stairs.

I don't remember much about fucking Veronica, only that she queefed a lot, made these little pussy farts. It was hard to find a rhythm with these sounds coming out; they embarrassed her. I wanted to say something, make a joke, like: *did someone step on a duck?* But I could see that wouldn't go over too well.

So we did our business: bang, bang, bang. The old human dance. We were both pretty disappointed: in ourselves, in our failure to feel something more. I'm not even sure I came. I might have faked it, and she didn't even bother. That's how it goes when you're young. The glands are there, functioning, reliable. It's the other stuff you can't rely on.

Really, the one I wanted was Betty. And Veronica wanted Rankin, no doubt. He was bigger and stronger, more at ease in his misbehavior.

We went downstairs. The door to the bedroom was ajar, and there was Rankin, his broad back winged out, pumping into Betty. With each thrust, she let out a little cry. Rankin looked like he did onstage, actually, his muscles all plumped up, rippled, shining with sweat. Veronica was behind me, watching, listening to her friend. We were about to back away, but Rankin must have known we were there because, without turning, he lifted his arm and waved us inside.

So we went and sat on the bed and watched them fuck. I'd seen Rankin naked plenty of times, in the showers at the gym, skinny dipping with Dana and the other girls. We were together so much that summer. And this just seemed like the logical extension: to see him in this context. I could smell the lotion he wore, some kind of aloe shit, and his hair gel. I was impressed with the articulation of his hip muscles.

Veronica was more focused on Rankin's cock. It was something to see: long, fat, with a swollen vein squiggling down the top, a scary, humbling thing, very much in scale with his body. I tried to focus on Betty. We could see the top half of her face when Rankin came out of her, her eyes half-shut, blonde curls falling across her cheek. The watching got us both worked up, and this time there was some heat involved.

So we had them side by side, on the same bed, Betty making her noises, Veronica queefing away, the tips of their hair touching on the bed sheet. At some point, Rankin and I looked at each other—we had turned at the exact same moment—and smiled, and we knew that our entire summer, in some way, had been building toward this. He made a signal with his hands, one index finger circling the other, and pulled back, out of Betty. And I did the same thing. We were quick about it.

Betty looked up at me as I lowered myself onto her. She was glassy-eyed, loose-mouthed. "Now what's all this?" she said, like she had caught us doing something naughty.

Veronica said, "Here comes the hit parade," and made a sound I'd not heard before, like she was easing into a cold lake.

The smell of sex was all around, their pussies, our cocks, spit mixed with bourbon and cigarettes and pot smoke, and beneath it all that faint sweetness of a woman's ass. It was so thick in that room, like a cape, or a veil.

Betty's body was smaller. I remember that. Her breasts bounced as we went at it, framed her chin, and when my hand slipped to her ass, her eyes seemed to clear for a moment and she nodded slowly.

Rankin wanted to take Veronica from behind. Her got her up on her knees, but the angle must have hurt her, because I could see her arm go up and she said, "No, wait, not that way." Rankin liked how she looked like that, though, and he knew what he wanted. He thrust his hips forward, and she let out a shriek.

Betty seemed roused for a second. She looked over. Veronica was wincing, and Betty said to her friend, so sweetly, "You look hot like that."

Then she and I were back into our thing, following the rhythm, and I felt her clinging to me, the inside of her, and she reached around and set her hand on my ass, to show me how she wanted it to happen. We got lost there for a while, and when we came out of it, Veronica was gone and Rankin was propped on his elbow, watching us and stroking his ridiculous cock.

"Where's Vicky?" Betty said softly.

"She went to get something," Rankin said. "Just us pros now."

Betty looked at Rankin, than at me, then at the door. "Bye bye baby," she said softly.

———————————

"I can tell you what I want," Rankin said.

Very little time had passed. I was still inside Betty, still touching her, slipping my finger inside her ass, enjoying that firm ring of warmth.

"I want that beautiful little mouth to kiss me."

Betty smiled. You could see, right then, how much attention she needed, how bottomless that need was in her.

"Get her on her knees," Rankin said. "Move her back a bit and get her on those knees, J. Good. Good. Now take her from behind."

I did as I was told. This was Rankin's show. It was his body we all wanted. Not the thing itself, in my case, but that variety of assurance. Or maybe it was more complicated. I was sort of mixed up.

I could see myself moving into Betty, the sweet curve of her backside dividing and rejoining, the dark, tiny folds of her. She made all the lovely noises she made. And then Rankin was on his knees, facing me, with Betty between us. He was leaning back against the headboard, and Betty was grappling with his cock, trying to fit the thing into her mouth. It kept slipping out. She was distracted. Her hand was around the base. She was trying to play with his balls, hanging on to them for balance practically.

Then I got fixed on that, her efforts to take him into her mouth, the ardency of her efforts, the sheen of him, her lips and cheeks distorting.

And there was a moment, just a moment, when our eyes met again, Rankin and me, and we leaned forward, slowly, both of us smirking at our good fortune, examining each other's muscles, as we did constantly, when we couldn't find a mirror, as if the other were really only a pleasing reflection of ourselves. His face got larger and larger and then our foreheads came together with a dull smack and we leaned against one another. We'd dropped our hands to our sides and though Betty was between us, though our cocks were safely tucked inside her, we both knew, at that very instant, that she was only a bridge connecting us. We were the ones in love, however it is that men love, that yearning for the final boundary, that sad blend of exuberance and terror. We weren't that way for very long, a second maybe, with all the blood roaring inside us, our lips so close, our noses, our tongues.

And I won't tell you that one or the other pulled away, made a joke, punched a shoulder. We were too excited and too ashamed of our excitement, and a little later on, we took all that out on Betty, going a little further than we should have with that poor, drunk girl, pushing too hard, pumping too hard, causing her pain that went beyond her want, which is when Veronica appeared and said, "Party's over guys."

They didn't leave immediately, though. This isn't one of *those* stories. It was Betty's car, you see, and she insisted on driving, so we had to get her sobered up. We took them out for a swim. The Atlantic was like a bathtub, and Betty floated there, under the stars, in her tank top, complaining about the sting.

That was the last night Rankin and I felt totally at ease together. We'd come too close to the edge, seen down to the filthy, unthinkable bottom of our love, and drawn back. And now, drawing back further, I can see how absurd we both were, mighty little muscle boys with cocks made of iron and hearts made of tin.

I stayed in Myrtle Beach through August, then took a bus back to Jersey and the safety of the first Mrs. Wrong. Rankin left not long after, drifted out to L.A. and, by his own account, did some work in the porn industry. He wrote me a postcard, promised to send along a tape. *Ass Angels 6*, something like that. Then it was carpentry, then stunt work, and when those didn't pan out, he decided to write a screenplay.

We only talked when things went seriously wrong, when the loneliness in us turned sharp. Often one or both of us were drunk. Eventually, we fell out of touch.

I did see him once more, a few years later. I was out in L.A. for a conference. I'd decided to go back to school and get my degree, which had led, somewhat inexplicably, to a job in pharmaceutical sales. Rankin was down in Venice Beach by then. I'd tried to call him a few times but gotten his machine. I assumed he was out on the beach, working out, strutting, trolling for tail. Good old Rankin. But I had his address from a postcard. And one night, bored out of my skull with cock-tail hour at the Sheraton, the idiotic drone of drug trials and commission schedules, I decided to pay him a visit.

I found the place, a little bungalow a few blocks from the beach. Nobody answered when I knocked, so I went to the car and got a pen and piece of paper and started to write out a note.

It began: *Hey fuckface!*

Then I heard that voice behind me. "Look at what the cat dragged in."

I turned, and there he was, old Rankin, in a wheelchair.

He was wearing fingerless gloves—what I thought of as his lifting gloves —and he still had the massive upper body, a few new tattoos. But his lower body just sort of disappeared into a baggy pair of jeans. He'd shaved his head, too, and I could make out the faint outlines of a bald spot. His eyes had sunk deep into their sockets.

I must have been staring, because Rankin cocked his head and said, "Surprise, surprise" just like Gomer Pyle.

I made some perfectly idiotic comment, greeting, whatever, as if we could just move right into the visit.

"You'll probably want to know why I'm a cripple," Rankin said.

Inside, he gave me the story, the basics anyway, just what you'd expect: driving late at night, drunk, spinal cord damage. "You know what the spinal cord is?" he said. "It's just jelly, J, a bunch of smart fucking jelly."

We were at his kitchen table by now. He talked a lot about the hospital, his rehab, his new program. He had the whole 12-step inspirational bullshit down pat, speaking with a great nervous vehemence. I couldn't see it then, but he was furious that I'd just shown up with no warning. My pity was about the meanest thing I could have done to him.

He wasn't drinking, so I couldn't drink, and pretty soon he announced that he had a meeting to attend.

"Sure," I said. "You need a lift?"

The word, just that single word, seemed to catch Rankin off guard. There was a long pause.

"You remember that night?" he said, finally.

"Which one?"

"You know the one."

I nodded.

"Those two girls, those crazy bitches." Something of the

old fire, his massive assurance, flickered. "They drove out there to get fucked that night, J. And they got fucked, did they not? Am I right?"

"That's what I remember."

"We should have filmed that shit."

"Sure."

He began to sing that old tune, "You Oughta Be in Pictures."

"I still see her sometimes," he said. "You know, that one little blonde, the Southern belle."

I was about to ask him how he'd tracked her down. Then I realized what he actually meant.

"What was her name?"

"Betty."

"Right. Betty. What a sweet little whore. Taking it from behind from you, sucking me off. Remember that? On Dana's bed. We should have filmed that shit." The way he said it, real guttural, I thought he might even be feeling turned on.

Then Rankin glanced down at his lap and shook his head. When he looked up again, his eyes were red. "Jesus, J, I gotta pee through a fucking tube."

I wanted to get up and embrace him, to consummate whatever we had started, all those years ago. But I was also afraid of him, his suffering, his sorrow, his abject lack of self-respect.

Anyway, he didn't wait around for me to work up the nerve. After a few seconds, he wheeled himself away from the table. That's what the gloves were for now. "I need to get ready for this thing," he said. "Sorry I can't hang longer."

"No problem," I said. "I'll give a call soon. Promise."

Then I felt compelled to add, "You're all right," which is when I knew he was a dead man, right then, pills, a gun, whatever it was going to be, the body was dead, the dream was dead, and I think I even approved of that plan. I did what most of us do, every day of our lives: I turned away. Got in the rental car, took to the highway, and there was the ocean, on my left, tugging at the dark shore, waiting for me to tell this story, to pretend such stories ever teach us anything, or ever end.

THE MARRYING KIND

Mary Anne Mohanraj

Chicago, 1980

"This isn't working." Leilani didn't say the words out loud, not with Jared working so hard, so earnestly, his large hands caressing her skin, his mouth traveling the hills and valleys of her body. It would have seemed cruel, after what felt like hours of his diligent efforts to arouse her laggard interest. It hadn't been hours yet, not tonight, but it wasn't the first night like this, oh no. After the first few nights of passion, Leilani had found it difficult to match Jared's interest, his attentions. It wasn't his fault—he was a nice man, intelligent, well read, attentive. He was exactly the kind of man she had thought she was looking for. And yet here they were in bed, and where there should have been a wet, urgent heat, there was nothing. Worse than nothing—a dry chill. Leilani was dry as a bone, dry as an old woman, and she was only thirty-four; it was too soon to be this cold and dry.

Her mother would have warned her, Leilani was sure, if her mother were still speaking to her, if her mother could have ever spoken so frankly of such things. This was the price Leilani paid for not marrying as a respectable girl would, for being restless, being wild. Her mother, born in another land, in another time, would say that her daughter had used herself up, and, despite her sensible self, Leilani felt a brief flicker of fear in her heart that maybe it was so. Maybe she had been too wild, for too long.

Thirty-four now—she had had sixteen years of love, men and women, passion and pleasure and joy and heartbreak and picking herself up and trying again. Not being willing to settle for just a nice lover, a good man, a kind woman—no, Leilani had seen the sad marriage her parents had had, the compromises of it, the costs. Instead, she had wanted it all, had wanted the thunder crash, the lightning strike that hit over and over and over again and told you that this one was worth fighting for. She had thought she had found it, more than once, but it had never quite worked out, and so here she was trying again, with Jared. Jared who was large and powerful and strong and even passionate, but always gentle with her, as if she were a flower that might be crushed under the weight of a pounding storm.

This wasn't working, and if she didn't have the heart to tell him so in bed, at least she could make the job easier for him and quicker for her. So the next time Jared slid down in the dark room, down to lick his way along her thighs, her calves, down to suck her toes, Leilani licked her own fingers and swiftly, sneakily slid them inside her, a quick motion, as practiced and familiar as scooping rice and curry off the plate and neatly into her mouth. This, at least, hadn't worn out, not yet, and a few quick strokes in exactly the right place was enough to raise her heartbeat, to bring her breath heavy into the summer-heated room, and that was enough for Jared, who came back up, and she almost wasn't quick enough moving her hand away, he almost caught her, but didn't. Then he was inside her, and it was wet enough, good enough for now, though a part of her felt sick at having used a whore's trick on the man. He was a good man. He deserved better.

Afterward, Leilani slipped out of bed, pulled on a thin cotton robe, left Jared sleeping. It was late, and they both had to get up early tomorrow for work. But she couldn't sleep on a night like tonight—it was thunderstorm weather, and they were overdue. The forecasters had been predicting a storm for weeks, but there had been nothing, nothing but the crackle in the air, the build-up that never quite discharged. It was driving her slowly mad. Leilani walked through the long, dark hallway, down past the dining room, the kitchen, following the same path on the ancient wooden floorboards that she had walked every night for the last week, heading out onto the back porch, out to where she could finally press her flesh against the wood railing, tilt her head back, gaze up and up at the dark sky, heavy with clouds that refused to give up their moisture. Not a star in sight.

It was so dark out here. She lived on the third floor, the top floor of the brownstone, and though her neighbors had back porches too, she could barely make out the outlines of them tonight. No one would see if she decided to touch herself here, to relieve the frustration that still coiled within her, that radiated out from her center to the tips of her fingers, the tips of her toes. Leilani could let the robe slip to the ground, could, naked in the night, mark a path across her skin with rough nails, dig fingers into flesh, leave bruises. She could fuck herself hard, here on this porch for all the world to see, because no one would see, fuck herself to exhaustion and satisfaction, with Jared safely asleep, never needing to know.

But she wouldn't do that, of course, because despite all her wildness, she wasn't that kind of girl—or at least, she wasn't any more. Sixteen years ago, she had let her first lover make love to her on a rooftop. Afterward, the world seemed full of possibilities, an adventure waiting in every open doorway. Leilani had hurled herself into love, opened her heart as wide as it could go. But there had been one failed affair after another, each one ending for a different reason, but always, heart-wrenchingly, ending. And with each one, Leilani became a little more careful, more cautious.

Until here she was with Jared, with no idea why she was with him. Leilani couldn't tell him what she wanted, what she needed, and she didn't think he could give it to her anyway. It was time, past time, to break things off and set him free.

Jared wanted to marry her. He had told her that the day they met, as she walked past him, walking down 57th Street to the bookstore. He was leaning against a tree, a burly black man with his head shaved, sharp in crisp white shirt and dark blue jeans. The kind of man her mother would cross the street to avoid. He whistled as she walked by. Leilani turned a little and smiled, appreciating the compliment, the lift to her spirits on a gray May morning, and he said, "A girl as pretty as you *must* be married." And she laughed, as much at being called a girl as anything else, here in Hyde Park, a campus town where pretty little eighteen-year-olds filled the tree-lined streets. She laughed, charmed, and had shaken her head no. And he smiled a wide smile of perfect shining teeth and said, "I sure would like to marry you myself." Leilani had thought he was joking.

Leilani hadn't said anything more to him that day, but she saw him again, a few days later, in the bookstore this time, two volumes of Tacitus tucked under one arm, and a third spread on the book-lined table before him. An English translation, not the original Latin, but still. His concentration so deep that he didn't even notice her walking past, and that had charmed her too, and made her ashamed that she had seen the rich, ebony shade of his skin and assumed that he was— well, not quite her kind, not the university, the intellectual, type. Later, over thick cheeseburgers and a shared chocolate milkshake at the Medici, she would discover that, in fact, Jared wasn't a grad student or a professor, that he did work in the physical plant, supervising the grounds crew, that he read ancient history for pleasure, for fun. That made it all the worse, of course. Sometimes Leilani thought that she had gone to bed with him a week later more out of embarrassment than anything else.

She admitted that to him the following night over dinner. Leilani had cooked, basmati rice and spicy chicken curry, sweet carrots and green beans with turmeric sauce. She wasn't much of a cook so she had to start over three times on the chicken curry, burning the onions the first time, scorching the meat the second. Leilani had been ready to scream with frustration, but had instead started over again, determined to finally, finally get it right. She had wished she could cook Jared a feast, an apology for what she'd been thinking. Over dinner that night, her eyes fixed on her half-eaten plate, the words fell awkwardly out of her mouth, "That first day, when we met— I didn't expect you to be smart. And when you asked me out, the only reason I said yes was because of the way you looked. Big. Strong." *Dark and dangerous.* She didn't quite have the nerve to say that last part, but the rest was bad enough. Leilani bit her lip, waiting for him to get angry, to storm out. It was what she deserved.

But instead, Jared was quiet for a long moment. Then he said, "Well, I suppose I didn't know much about you when I saw you walking down that street. I knew you had that long black hair, so silky smooth, and I wanted to swim in it, like swimming in the ocean, at night." He reached out, across the table, took a few strands of her hair in his fingertips and tugged them, gently, making her look up at him. His eyes were calm, thoughtful. "I knew your skin was like sweet coffee with cream." Jared smiled then, that smile that had captured her the day they met. Smiled and said, with a sweet lilt in his voice, a sudden, deep, down-home accent, "But now that I know you a little, I surely do like you, Miss Leilani. And I think you like me too."

And Leilani had laughed, charmed by his speech, and by him, and admitting that it was true, that she did like him, liked the way he talked, the way he walked. She liked that Jared called his mother every night, just for a few minutes, just to say hello. Leilani liked that he could beat her at chess, which none of her lovers ever had. She liked that he could cook like a demon, that he made her johnny cakes with sweet honey, and barbecued ribs so tender that the flesh fell right off them. She especially liked that Jared had eaten everything that she had cooked, never saying a word of complaint about the chicken that still, despite all her efforts, managed to taste more than a little burnt. He was a good man, the kind of man you fell in love with, the kind of man you married. There was no good reason to think that he might not be the man for her.

At first, the sex had been good too.

————————————

The first night she brought him upstairs to her bed, as she unbuttoned Jared's white shirt, uncovering solid muscle over layers of more muscle, Leilani felt like it was her birthday, Christmas, even her wedding day, all rolled up into one. Jared was the best present ever. Six feet tall and so strong that he could pick her up with one arm. Over a week of dinners, and alone in her bed after, she had closed her eyes and slid her hand under the covers, between her legs. She had made herself crazy with fantasies of just how he would take her, how he would lose control, would slam her down into the bed, would ravage her willing body. And at first, he had seemed ardent enough, had covered her in kisses. Jared had traced long, slow paths from mouth to collarbone, from breast to nipple, and then eagerly down to the triangle between her thighs.

Leilani had been wet that night, had been hungry for him, had spread her legs and invited him in with no hesitation at all. And when she finally had him inside her that first night, when he began to move, sending shivers through her, Leilani had raked her nails down his back, bit the flesh of his shoulder hard. Jared didn't complain—he'd taken it, taken everything she could dish out—but he didn't reciprocate. That night had been good enough, but it had made her nervous. And as she'd feared, no matter what she did to him, that night or the ones that followed, he was unfailingly gentle with her. Jared whispered sweet words in her ear. He said softly, "I could really love you, girl." Or even, "You're the kind of girl I'd like to marry." And then he kissed her again, softly, on the lips. He kissed her with respect, and it made her want to scream.

Leilani told herself, "Well, he just needs to get to know me better." But the nights and weeks went by, and though she whispered, "faster," "harder," Jared didn't seem able to take the hint. She hadn't been able to just come right out and say, "I need you to fuck me really hard." So maybe it was her fault that it hadn't gotten better—it had gotten worse. Until now, here they were.

For the last few weeks, the best part of dating Jared hadn't been when they were alone together—it was when they were out. They walked to campus and Leilani defiantly held his hand, enjoying the covert glances and outright stares. They went to restaurants together; they cuddled close in movies. At the Reynolds Club, they ate lunch with her professor friends on his break—then after he'd kissed her and left, Leilani smiled mysteriously at their fevered questions. *What's he like? Is he really on the grounds crew? This isn't serious, is it? What will your parents say?*

That one did make her heart thump, though she wasn't about to show it. By now, her parents would have heard the news from someone; her sisters would have discussed it all in detail; her father the professor might even have seen them, walking around campus, holding hands. But her parents hadn't spoken to her in years, so unless Leilani asked her sisters, she needn't know what they were saying. Someday her parents might speak to her again. Maybe if she got married. Maybe even if she married Jared. Her parents were educated people—they might be furious at their daughter, ashamed of her, for flagrantly having sex outside of marriage, but they would never admit, even to themselves, that they didn't want her to marry a black man.

At least Jared's family was honest.

Jared had begged Leilani to go with him to his sister's birthday party; begged with words, with soft touches to the back of her neck, with wide, dark eyes, until she would have found it easier to kick a puppy than say no to him. So Leilani had put on a sleeveless white dress, modestly knee-length, had brushed out her hair until it shone, and, at his request, wore it loose and long. She had let him drive her west, past the university, into the areas where the students weren't supposed to walk. When they got out of the car, he'd put out his arm and she had slipped a hand through it, so that they might parade up the front walk to his mother's neat little house, cheerful with a fresh coat of yellow paint.

Leilani had been on display, and that was to be expected— she was the new girlfriend. What she hadn't expected was the way the men looked at her, with more concentrated lust than she'd ever experienced, an honest intensity of desire. They said to her face, *Girl, you are fine! Do you have any sisters?* Leilani blushed, and Jared grinned wide, showing bright white teeth, shepherding her around with a proprietary hand on the small of her back. She could have handled the men, but then there were the women. Jared's mother, polite but cold. Jared's sister, Kesia, whose skin was even darker than Jared's, and who neatly managed, with a plateful of food and a cold lemonade, to avoid shaking her hand. When Leilani went to use the washroom, she emerged to overhear Kesia hissing to Jared, angry and low, *What, you couldn't get a white girl, so you settled for next best?* And fury rose in Leilani, fury rose and then died, smothered by the knowledge that if Jared had picked her to satisfy some tainted craving, she had done worse.

"What are you doing out here?" Jared leaned in the doorway, his voice low and rough, his body huge and dark and menacing—or it would be, if it were her fantasy. But she knew him too well for that. Leilani fought to keep the frustration from her voice as she said, "I couldn't sleep. Go back to bed. No need for both of us to be tired tomorrow."

"You should come inside—it's going to storm."

"They keep saying that, but it never happens. It drives me crazy."

He was quiet a long moment. Then said, "Are you talking about the storm, or about us?"

She hadn't realized that he knew how frustrated she was. Leilani had underestimated him again, but she was too angry to be embarrassed this time. Not that she had any right to be angry at him—he hadn't done anything wrong. It wasn't his fault that he was just too nice. The kind of guy she should be with, not the kind she wanted.

"This isn't working for me. I'm sorry, Jared." What else could she say? *It isn't you, it's me?* Hard for anyone to believe that, and not much comfort even if you did. At least she was ending it early, before anyone could get too hurt. It had only been a few weeks.

He was quiet for a long time. Then, finally, "You're not giving us much of a chance."

Leilani wrapped her arms around herself, not wanting to see the lostness in his eyes. Maybe she'd been fooling herself, about no one getting hurt. Maybe it was too late. Maybe it had been too late from that first day, when he said he'd like to marry her. She wasn't the marrying kind.

"I think it's better this way. I do." It wasn't really about the sex. The sex was just a symptom. Jared was a sweet guy. But Leilani needed more than sweetness.

"Well then." Heavy acceptance in his voice, and she was glad he wasn't going to fight her on this. Wasn't she? "Come inside at least. It's starting to rain."

A fat drop hit her arm, hard. And then another, and another. In less than a minute, the sky had opened up with the suddenness that you only found in a summer thunderstorm, and the rain was pounding down, wind whipping it along, and she was already drenched. Slamming into her skin, blinding her, washing away all kinds of dirt and darkness. Leilani felt her heart lift, her pulse speeding up, racing. The rain was talking to her, telling her what she needed to do. One last chance.

"You go ahead," she said quietly. "I want to stay out here. Just for a little while."

"Your clothes are getting soaked!"

"Then I'll take them off," Leilani said, fighting back the urge to laugh. It wouldn't be kind, laughing now. But, oh, her body wanted to, and that had nothing to do with Jared, and everything to do with the rain, with the sharp crack of thunder and the lightning that whited out the sky a moment later. Leilani slipped out of her robe and let it fall to deck, leaning back now against the railing again, closing her eyes, letting the warm rain pound against her face, her breasts, her belly. It was a good body to give to the night. No longer as slim as when she was the girl who liked to run, but with an added lushness now, curves that flashed in the lightning light and then disappeared again into darkness.

Were there neighbors watching the storm, safe behind their windows? Watching her? Leilani didn't care. Let them hide inside and watch. Ah, *there* was the rush, the excitement she'd been missing. There was the part of herself she had lost. Leilani lifted her hands, cupped her breasts, dug her fingers into flesh. Felt shivers race beneath her skin as she squeezed her nipples between her fingertips. Was he watching? If Jared could walk away from *this,* then she'd know she was right to send him away.

"Damn, you're crazy, girl." Finality in his voice, and the screen door slamming, and silence after. *Ah, well,* Leilani thought. She'd tried her best. Maybe her best wasn't what Jared wanted. It hurt, but the pain slid into the hard, wet wood against her back, the water-logged tendrils of her hair whipping in the wind, the slick trail her fingers followed down her body, down her belly, to that promised land she had lost sight of.

And then the door slammed again, and Jared was there, one big hand grabbing her wrists, pulling them up, hard, above her head, to press against a post. The other hand on her flesh, hard and rough, not bothering with soft touches, long lingerings. Straight between her thighs, pressing her legs apart, shoving fingers up, inside, and, god, she was wet. Not just with rain. A few quick strokes and then Jared's hand was gone, leaving an aching emptiness; her hips arched up, involuntary, and, thank god, thank god he was there to meet her. Naked as well, soaking wet and completely hard, his hand on her ass, lifting her up and onto him, so that her legs wrapped around him as far as they could go. Her hands still high above her head, her wrists still crushed in his grip, and it hurt, and that just made it better. He fucked her hard against the post, no gentleness left in him. She was racing now, racing the storm, and the storm was going to win, but that was fine, that was great. The lightning flashed, the thunder crashed, and she whited out in a shock that ran from head to toes to fingertips.

Afterward, they lay together on the deck as the storm dwindled down, down to a few warm raindrops, here and there. Jared was solid beside her, warm. Her wrists ached, and so did other parts. Lots of other parts. There might be splinters in her back.

Jared rolled away, and for a chilly moment Leilani thought that he was going to get up, going to walk away, disgusted with them both, leaving her a used, crumpled heap on the wooden deck. There was always that possibility. A necessary risk. But he just rolled far enough away to raise up on one elbow, his thigh still pressed warm against hers, his dark eyes looking down at her. Smiling. Jared asked her then, his voice rough with what might have been anger, or passion, or laughter, "So was *that* enough to satisfy you, girl?"

Leilani just smiled back, not sure of her answer. She reached up and pulled him down into a kiss. The storm was over, but there were many hours left until morning. *Maybe,* Leilani thought, her heart still pounding, her throat dry, *or maybe not.*

About the Authors

THOMAS S. ROCHE's books include *His, Hers, Dark Matter*, and the *Noirotica* series. His short stories have appeared in more than 300 Web sites, magazines, and anthologies, including several volumes of the *Best American Erotica* and *Best New Erotica* series. In his spare time, he keeps a weblog and dabbles in fetish photography. You can keep track of him at www.skidroche.com.

RACHEL KRAMER BUSSEL (www.rachelkramerbussel.com) is Senior Editor at *Penthouse Variations* and a Contributing Editor at *Penthouse,* where she writes the "Girl Talk" column. Her "Lusty Lady" column runs biweekly in *The Village Voice,* and she's the editor of *Naughty Spanking Stories from A to Z 1* and *2*. Her writing has been published in more than 70 anthologies, including *Best American Erotica 2004* and *2006*, and in *AVN, Bust, Gothamist, Mediabistro,* the *New York Post*, and *Time Out New York.*

MIKE KIMERA was raised as an Irish Catholic in England and now works as a management consultant in Switzerland. At the age of forty-three, he started writing stories about sex and lust and the things they do to us, and five years later he's still at it. *Writing Naked*, a collection of his stories, was published in 2005.

Queer girl sex is a favorite flavor of erotica for DEBRA HYDE, more of which can be found in *Best Lesbian Erotica 2004* and *2006*, *The Good Parts: Pure Lesbian Erotica*, and *Stirring Up a Storm: Tales of the Sensual, the Sexual, and the Erotic*. Her BDSM fiction appears in *Best Bondage Erotica 2* and both volumes of *Naughty Spanking Stories from A to Z*. When she isn't dreaming about (or engaging in) sex, she's writing about it at her long-running weblog, Pursed Lips.

CECILIA TAN is the author of numerous erotic books and short stories, including *Black Feathers, The Velderet,* and *Telepaths Don't Need Safewords*. Her work has appeared in *Best American Erotica, Ms. Penthouse,* and everywhere in between. She has also edited dozens of anthologies of erotic fiction for Circlet Press, Masquerade Books, Blue Moon Books, and others, including *Blood Surrender, Sextopia,* and *Erotic Fantastic*. Find out more at www.ceciliatan.com.

SIMON SHEPPARD is the author of *In Deep: Erotic Stories, Kinkorama: Dispatches From the Front Lines of Perversion,* and *Sex Parties 101*. His work has also appeared in more than 125 anthologies, including many editions of *Best Gay Erotica* and *Best American Erotica,* and he's the author of the columns "Sex Talk" and "Perv." He lives in San Francisco and hangs out at www.simonsheppard.com.

SHANNA GERMAIN's erotic stories have appeared or are scheduled to appear in dozens of publications and anthologies, including *Best Bondage Erotica 2, Dykes on Bikes, The Good Parts, Heat Wave,* and *Rode Hard, Put Away Wet*. You can see more of her work, erotic and otherwise, on her Web site, www.shannagermain.com.

CHEYENNE BLUE combines her two passions in life and writes travel guides and erotica. Her erotica has appeared in several anthologies, including *Best Women's Erotica, Mammoth Best New Erotica, Best Lesbian Erotica*, and *Best Lesbian Love Stories*, and on many websites. Her travel guides have been jammed into many glove boxes underneath the chocolate wrappers. She divides her time between Colorado, USA, and Ireland and is currently working on a book about the quiet and quirky areas of Ireland. You can read more of her erotica on her Web site, www.cheyenneblue.com.

MICHAEL HEMMINGSON recently co-edited *Expelled from Eden: A William T. Vollmann Reader*. He is the author of the novels *The Rose of Heaven, Melody, The Rooms*, and *Amateurs,* a novelization of his story "Movements," which appeared in the first *Aqua Erotica*. He lives in San Diego.

BILL NOBLE is an award-winning writer and poet from Northern California and longtime fiction editor of the premier online magazine of literary erotica, Clean Sheets. His work appears in venues ranging from *Best American Erotica* to *New Millennium Writings*. More information may be had at www.billnoble.net.

STEVE ALMOND is the author of two story collections, *The Evil B.B. Chow* and *My Life in Heavy Metal,* and the nonfiction book *Candyfreak*. His various perversions may be inspected at www.bbchow.com.

MARY ANNE MOHANRAJ is the author of *Bodies in Motion,* a set of Sri Lankan–American linked stories (July 2005, HarperCollins). She teaches at Vermont College and Roosevelt University and is working on a follow-up book, *The Arrangement,* a contemporary threesome novel. She is the Executive Director of DesiLit (www.desilit.org) and of the Speculative Literature Foundation (www.speclit.org).